First Montag Press E-Book and Paperback Original Edition October 2013

Montag Press 978-0-9822809-9-7
Cover art © 2013 Arnopeopledesign.com
Cover design © 2013 Arnopeopledesign.com

Montag Press Team:
Project Editor – Alexandra Paskulin
Layout & E-Book Designer – Badger McInnes
Managing Director – Charlie Franco

A Montag Press Book
www.montagpress.com
Montag Press
536 E. 8th Street
Davis CA, 95616 USA

Montag Press, the burning book with the hatchet cover, the skewed word mark and the portrayal of the long-suffering fireman mascot are trademarks of Montag Press.

Printed & Digitally Originated in the United States of America
10 9 8 7 6 5 4 3 2 1

AGAINST

DECLAN TAN

MONTAG

For Vera

власть дается только тому, кто посмеет наклониться и взять ее.

– Достоевский, *Преступление и наказание*

Zur Tür kommt man noch. Knie hat man noch, in der Tür ist es besser. Verflucht! Draußen muß es hell sein."

– Brecht, *Baal*

PART ONE

Iris Out

CHAPTER ONE

(EXT. STREET - DAWN)

I looked up into the sky. A heavy gray pregnant with rain. I lit the first cigarette.

Think. I'd been kicked out or I'd left. I couldn't remember which. Imagining her sitting up there, breathing in her fine cigarettes, stiff and ignoring emotion. The red stream and broken smoke.

(INT.)

She said she couldn't stand me for my inconsistency. I said: one is not the same throughout the day. One cannot be. One should not be.

(EXT. STREET - DAWN)

Stood in the breeze craning my neck to see, I waited. Taking whatever angle I could to subsist. I spied it, through the unborn limbs of the cherry blossom, the window shifting through the branches all emptied of leaves.

(INT.)

It could be the end of me.

(EXT. STREET - NIGHT)

The view of the aged edifice remained flat. Cold. Solid and dead. I had no tricks to disregard that. I couldn't deceive my self to even those little things. At least not completely. Not yet.

The gray climbed and swayed between the clouds. Like her it gleamed without remorse. I waited outside for something to happen. A signal from the window. A solemn face. Some gesture of regret. I hoped that maybe she might change her mind.

I waited there for a long time. Not realising there was nothing left in her to change.

I waited, waited
motionless but my vision unsteady
heavy from the brew
tree bending with the wind
as if to pick me up
in its bony grip.

But nothing came. Nothing took me. So I left. I moved ahead down the swollen street looking once over my shoulder.

Still nothing, only the hollow sound of bronchiolar branches reaching across, breathing in-out. I walked along head down with the world now opening its mouth to me. Maybe one day she would believe that I had become something.

Someone that asked the right questions.

Maybe one day I would believe that too.

(INT.)

The widening jaw of the high streets and parades swallowed the laces and leather bound to my feet. I walked farther away from her into the open city.

Laid between grotesque boutiques with every uniquely uniform man-woman-and-child's growing baggage, clanging, bouncing between them, the path rolled out its dark purple tongue beneath my shoes. Flashing past were the carefully moulded catchphrases and passwords of our culture, drawn up in some long beige room, along a heavy mahogany table, surrounded by the sane, all the way around. Bags struck at the eyes of beggars, swung low at arm's length.

Watching others plunder it all is different to watching your self do the same. Like she said: subjective with others, objective with self.

But she was mistaken. She wouldn't be so smug when the glass came crashing in, I thought. They stormed the breach, the material legion, their final battle, consuming along the way, hunting for the kill, a lunch of charred flesh in one hand, and the handle of a bulging sack to weigh down the other. The balancing act of the mediocre, the Old Man once called it. Keeping everything alive and dying as they went, eating and killing it all along the cobbled street. Keeping it all in the Zero state. And the most hor-

rific thing they could imagine was someone not noticing them, someone not watching while they plundered it all. All the amateur stars of an indifferent sky.

The sound of their treads on cobblestone. An unmistakable march. Rubber on stone. A familiar echo. I watched their legs swing in the afternoon light. Where aggressiveness and competition had once proven useful, exponentially grown populations now painted high the giant, rotten question mark.

(EXT. BEDROOM - NIGHT)

I lifted the pen and watched black ink soak the page. Crawling out its wet web. I looked hard at the words. Check the spelling. I squinted. I know what's in my head. Inside. Outside. It's all the same.

Remember, most actions are the result of learning. Obsessions like correct spelling. But the original thought, the original action comes from unlearning. Dispelling.

(INT.)

The parents with their children slipped by, the parents dressed as their children, or their children dressed as their parents. Though I pondered, I couldn't decide which might be worse. So I simply watched them plunging their Selves and each other into the sliding mud. Across the way sat a woman, paper before her. Her hand moving across the page. A pencil, ink, an idea spread across it? I moved closer, and instead saw the headlines. The angles. The options: Create/Delete. The angle is a lie. The angle is a convenience.

I stood there sweating. Rested against a low wall. Hand resting upon its edge. My long raincoat too heavy to bear. And I felt a mass of eyes on me. Wanting not to draw more attention by making any rash moves, I endured the strong hot flushes. Drenching my arms. My face pulsing. I froze, avoiding life.

(EXT. CITY STREET - DAY)

The generations and empires aged and withered with time, the young fodder brought up as droning brand buyers of the future, wound up and pointed at the next crippled tower, the next craze, the next, the next. Loyal and ideological. Minds tyrannised. Children and men blurring past on wheels, all manner: scooters, skates, wheels on shoes, too fast and too busy to notice the rubble falling from above. Terrorised. Destroyed. Looking up to the state, the parent, the god, for guidance. For solutions. Given something, finding nothing.

Live by the rule: the Master is everything, the subject nothing.

Moving along the Progressive Alliance, the Coalition, for the build of a silent history so ritually obsessed with money that even some fictionalised depiction of one of us squandering some large amount, or flittering it away unnecessarily, could send us into a rage; phantasies forcing an ache through the stomach, a fleeting misery that an opportunity for victory had passed us by. Forcing us to remember and at the same time forget. Through the medium. Through the message.

Options: Create/Delete.

(INT.)

No. No good. Not alive yet. Can't introduce her like that. Too languid. And such bitterness. Stop preaching. It smells of farts. You don't get ideas across like that, you need laughs. How predictable to moan about economics/politics. How very grimly predictable.

Don't mix the words so forcefully. I mean, you've probably told yourself whether you want to like it or not by now. The letters, they're cluttering up and falling over each other.

Do something. Do something. Bleed it out.

Burn some of the fat off.

(EXT. CITY STREET - DAY)

The places the pueblo once worked and the status they used to hold, as pillars of an industrial society, people as pedals stepped on to put the wheel in motion, holding up the iron and the steel with dirty hands. Where huge run-

down factories once lay in the hinterlands, hollowed out, now stood the shiny new image. A placebo culture where everything mattered and nothing counted. Gone were the grime, the dripping dirt and snaking filth that bred misery and struggle.

Land where earnestness once stood now gripped monuments to trickle-down opulence, luxury dribbled from the heavens, onto the windless landscape of post-literate post-industry post-society: fashion stores, department shopping, all day-night bonanzas of music, art, literature, all products For Sale Now – smeared multicolour streaks breaking the sky to stand opposed against the long uninterrupted period of darkness hurtling forward, puncturing our once-rubicund hearts and turning us out, emptied, as unwanted but necessary loose change; passive receptors and empty vessels filled by charging mass producers. Tacticians on the street pounded and caged by the strategists of the rooftops, a marginality held strong by its spreading through the brain and the string, through the heart and the cracks in the pavement.

(INT.)

No, no. Try again. Too ominous, too earnest. Who'll read that? They'll close the lid on that in a second. Give them some relief, give them some escapism. Some pleasure, some excitement. Distraction.

Diversion god damn it.

(EXT. CITY STREET - DUSK)

I walked through the cobbled streets. Buildings, brick upon brick, gray upon gray, stretched up to the clouds. Bags emblazoned with boutique labels pulsated (no, sagged) in death grips. Handles?

They balanced on the scales of injustice, frozen mullions...

(INT.)

Same thing. Too conscious. Always too conscious, go to sleep.

Too cerebral. Never alive, never free.

Were *they* like this? Did *they* worry like this?

Stop that.

Push it with some meaning. No. Go to the borderline.

CHAPTER TWO

From across the avenue he had seen the man pacing the floor in the opposing apartment. The man had looked down at his feet as he spoke. Reasoning something. Gesticulating with his arms and cursing the four walls. Crying out at the mirror. Cursing himself. First he would take three steps from left to right. A gaping stride covering the small living room. Turning on his heel he made his way back, his chest heaving.

He rubbed his dry eyes. They were beginning to fail him. He thought that this was a bad sign. They were becoming unreliable. Weak and blurred. He struggled to differentiate the colour from the form. Looking up again he saw a silent wind blowing on the outer side of the glass. The fatigued tree branches leaning to one side. The gray-brown of the bark showing its age.

He laid down the pen and looked again. Out of the glass. Out of the room. Out of his eyes.

PART TWO

Black

Iris In

CHAPTER ONE

(INT.)

I wanted to smoke a cigarette in all the places I had wanted to smoke a cigarette in that city.

So I visited all of them one by one. I took my coat from the back of the chair and made steps away from the desk. That dead heap of boards. I picked up the last fresh pack and slipped them in the left inside pocket, checking the right for my lighter. Why was that important? For some reason these details seemed important.

I walked out the door, clicking it shut behind me.

(EXT. CITY SIDE STREET - NOON)

From where do we get our models for living? From where do we find acceptability?

In a far off land, I make my self a home.
I am weak, yet wield force and power.
I am lost, yet stand tall atop a stage.
I rise when night falls.
And when I rise, I have a great fear of sinking.

(INT.)

The Clock stops.

CHAPTER TWO

He sits watching through the window as the tree begins to edge its way down, leaning heavily and dipping down to the road. The leaves and branches brush pavement and windshield together as one. Gentle. Scratching the surfaces.

He refocused his vision. He could not see her in there. Her head had dropped, though he felt she was close. Against the wall. Still near. There had been a dispute, an angry exchange. He was not yet sure what had passed in that room but he kept his face inches from the glass and waited.

The window caught his breath and swallowed it in.

(INT.)

And The Clock ticks.

I stood, puffing and lighting again, vicious hand to mouth resuscitation, cancer smoking cancer. Cultivating the habit of punctuating every event, and every non-event, in my life. I stood and watched the people from under bland sculptures commissioned by the city council, designed in some aboveground office by a team of lawyers and a group of professionals sat round a long boardroom meeting table. Who designed the stick man? I suspected it was them. Inoffensive and sexless. Like gods designing the eunuch of ages, to toy with, to confound. Urging and vomiting out directions, instructions, sick words while hands worm and turn their crude enterprise.

In this life we have everything backward. Born into death. Politeness before truth. The suicidal earth sets itself alight. And just as how death comes before life for some of us, man does not work because *he* has something to offer the world. Instead he is forced to work because he is told something can be offered to *him*. Forced to cultivate a personality beneficial to the slow suicide of the Earth. And where do we find acceptance? Always in another, always external. Rarely in these conditions could we hope to find it within. And we are taught many things out of blindness. We are told some are born for Greatness. We are told some have Greatness thrust upon them. This too is backward. Most, if not all, have Idiocy thrust upon them. And then, again, some are born to it. And one day there will be no bone left to grind. Some speckled wind will blow its heavy breath across our vision and over our trees and leave us all in the hollow.

Or is it not us but simply the murderous sun that has forsaken us? I lit a rotten cigarette and watched its burning ember glow, the ash over-running its edge until the small orange hum of heat was lost in the gray-black. I blink and wash my eyes with sparse tears.

The foreign body sensation.

We create problem solvers to problems we ourselves have created. Is man just a cancer on this earth? It cannot be. By its nature it has given birth to the footprint of man. So is it the Sun and the Universe and all its trappings that have laid this mighty circle of beginning-end? I watch a man unload six-foot-high boxes from a truck and wheel them through the door of a high-street clothing store. Every step I watch closely. And I see the wheel turn. I see him heaving and huffing out breath. I wonder if the earth is killing itself. Every move he makes he unravels a little further the trail for our final neutrality. The Earth is set alight, by what, by itself or by all the spontaneously combined conditions of all nature? Of physics and science? The conditions of its existence determine its fate. Death. And the same is graphed for mankind. Does the Earth feel us as some foreign body sensation? Or as a part of its own skin? Its own loose flesh. He wheels out the next set of boxes.

As I watch the small wheels turn I'm reminded of her repetition theory. This design, filling this box, now fashionable, now modern, would have behind it the same idea one hundred years from now. Slogans would tell us, by living vicariously through the shining and straightened hairs on our society's head, that we were succeeding if *they* were succeeding. The people walk by, looking in through windows of shops not yet open. Having desire fed to them and feeding back their own with some secret poison laid inside to boot. Write the Future, we are told. Taught to live in emptiness, and happily, as the future is written for us. Besieged by manufactured perversity. Depending where you looked, something meaningless took prominence over something potentially meaningful. Sport reaching the front pages. Showbiz and gossip clawing across and through it all. Paranoia that these things were happening. No. Not paranoia. Awareness. The awareness reduced to the simplistic label of paranoia. The state could close in on us, but to notice it would be paranoia. Or was it awareness of the possibility?

We had clicked on to the last suffering cycle of change. From now on it would be all neo-this neo-that, all regurgitated and repeated, re-combined to form something simultaneously old and new: new-old.

I clenched my fist and looked at the lost ink on the knuckles. Every writer is part of a movement, regardless of whether they accept it or are aware of it. The so-called Great Novels of every century, it is a fact, were not written hundreds of years before, no. The process is an evolution, a movement. A mass of writers makes up the flood. How much we put down to individual writers is up to the reader. Even the novels or the work supposedly revolutionary merely reverses or turns on its head the form, the meaning and the structure, the content. Merely reversed and therefore still made of the same basic ingredients. In the same way fashion had clicked, in the same way design had clicked, in the same way art had clicked, the old repeating as the new, writing was making the clicking sound in my ear as it dripped out.

Subjective without message other than that created by the viewer, the consumer, as we lock ourselves in, closing all the doors and sealing them shut. Producing our own mirrors and *being* mirrors simultaneously. Projecting our Selves onto it, into it. The reflection more thrilling than the reality. Reflecting ego and self, bringing it all back to the cracked mirror of our own image which echoed off and repeated as far as we let it.

To infinity.

Divided sunlight shone into the kaleidoscope where creativity had been distilled into the holy moment of creator, rather than any focus on the creation itself, refracting back the sorry and turgid intellectuals all specialised in their locked offices, where we have been left with homilies of ideologising from the top of the class down. Yes we were all individual, yes we were all unique. But eventually we're all put through the sieve, and then we pour out as easily classifiable characters.

So then what are you? I said.

Mute. She laughed.

It was just a theory.

In another hundred years modern art will not have changed. That evolution has ended. The only remaining morsel of popular art will be self-referential masturbation from here on in. Stuck on repeat, no progress. Where paint and canvas used to say something unspeakable, it now only reflects back to the dark room. Showing us only what we wanted or were capable of seeing. So-called poets of matter would be like all the unsuccessfuls, and like me. Trying it through failing. It would just go over and over like fashionable clothing, like women's magazines printing doctrines on 'real-life' stories, health, food, homes, gardens, interiors: dead beasts but somehow breathing. The same things in new combinations. Nothing fresh. Nothing original. But what ever was? Try to create something new and with a little scratching around you realise it's most likely already been done. Leave it too long and it expires quickly. Though what was being sold didn't need to be original or fresh, just the next rung on the endless ladder down to the shit.

Amnesia was setting in for all of us. It was a new Age of it. Soon we would completely forget who we were, what we were meant to do, and how. It doesn't take an abstraction to help you look at something in a new way, there are some that can do it. And there are others that can't.

(EXT. BEDROOM - DAY)

He stewed the pot with green and bilious yellows sticking to the spoon and the edges. Needed more boiling, until it slipped off the wooden spatula. He pumped the heat with a twist on the gauge and the mixture slopped and poured off as it bubbled inward and deeper. The vat almost ready for consumption, he took a sip from the wooden spoon and turned around. Sitting upright. Banisteriopsis caapi. Ayahuasca. Dimethyltryptamine. DMT. All in the swollen future room.

He drank some back, tipping it into his head; he gripped the bucket, looking up the crying wall with bloodshot eyes.

(INT.)

Before her eye, she held her hand
steady, dangling
the needle
on a string.
His typing in the next room cracked
out through the hallway,
the walls of opportunity
closing in,
through a door
forcing her utmost concentration.
For her it was a noise
impossible to ignore.
She could try
to sleep now

but
it would be futile.
He would soon come in,
the keys still in her ears,
to see
what
she was
doing.

(EXT. STREET – AFTERNOON)

I lit another, feeling trite. Smokers could be just as dreadfully tiresome as the rest. Reverse self-righteousness was the law with them, preaching something like the Welcoming of Death, the acceptance of mortality. Well, the acknowledgement of it at least. But still, we all latched on to something, and sometimes it'd be plain contradiction, and that'd be enough. The double life of depravity. Everyone had a phase with the life-death repetition cycle sooner or later. Whether they called it midlife or quarter-life or half-life, all the decay was set in motion the instant the crying started. You don't have to die to commit suicide. Most haven't. It only takes a small piece frittered into black to turn all the rest that way. Maybe even just wanting it was enough for it to be effective. Maybe just a vision of the self from the outside, the external, bringing the empty out.

(INT.)

I lit another. For every person that unsettled me, I smoked a cigarette.

The plain angles of public pubic art shielded any light from shining in on me. I stood, looking up to find some sunbeam leaning in. Cosmic rays energising the ether. The ether doesn't exist. Where did it go if you moved something into it? Still there, I thought. Available for filling, by anything old or new. Dead or alive. Does it displace if a chair is moved? A bookshelf? What about a moving person. I was the ether then, wasn't I? *Writing this, I was.*

I had smoked the pack and started to search around my coat and pockets for more.

The people glided around me, blathering, screeching the same words as the next and the one before. Without pause. Without thought.

Again, again.

I observed.

Placing the candy apple in the middle and watching all creatures swarm on it. That's what they do. That's what I have to do if I am to survive. It's called success. Pitiful.

The Worms protrude from the rotten apple. Created equal but not the same. Escaping fear is the rule in our life and times, but only by moving closer towards it do we feel it evaporate. The only thing we can face now is ease and ignorance.

More time, more speed, fast, faster, optimum efficiency is what they want. Cradle to grave in straight lines. More trivia, more data. Unattainable aims. Weaving games and lies with God's honest truths. And Manfred wanting to reinvent the candied apple. Grow it from the tree, drop it in the sugar, place it high above for all the insects to look at, to create the new epidemic of the people.

I sat for a while and thought, writing the book in my head, the words swimming around in there. Professionalism stifled creativity. It stifled revolution. Like dragging some dead animal up the road. The years of abuse had left me cold and isolated. I had to use their language and put the words together in a new way, to conjure some meaning, to lay the lines across the page like I was laying track. Something new to walk on. Or rail for some new train to ride.

But I was just another one in the long row of infinite monkeys tapping away on one of the infinite typewriters, if only for my self, my own ego, to discover my own ignorance, rather than extol any 'way' that we all should follow.

(EXT. CITY PARK - DAY)

I walked to the edge of the parkway, standing at its gate. A painted steel rail ran along the perimeter, darkened by pigeon droppings. The benches sparsely filled. The grass inhabited by beast and bird. Picnicking

couples crumbled biscuits and crackers over the lawn.
An old man perched on the edge of a secluded bench.
Surrounded by a small, dedicated flock of pigeons, he
feeds them his breakfast and theirs. He scatters crumbs
to those furthest; the eager and bold hover around his
shoes, hoping for the best of it. He mumbles laughter
and choice words through a gray goatee as he watches
them scrounging and chasing the crust. He breathes solemn breaths. His fingers roughly rip the dough in the
paper bag. A scurry for the stolen luncheon.

(INT.)

*Sitting behind a granite wall, he spent the jobless hours
watching people go by, the people practicing for years who
or what they were meant to be. Who they wanted to be
or how others wanted them to be, holed up in Suburbiton. They were the half-smoked cigarettes, soaked in the
ashtray. They were the broken matches. He watched them
as the clothed but uncivilised animals they were, eyeing
them from above, seeing them scatter and cry amongst
the trees and the cement, unconsciously chasing the black
cloud when the rains came. And he looked in on himself
doing the same, doing it through the page, tapping tip tap
at the well of the self, just as worthless, just as desperate
to embody something that wasn't merely his body. What
was it they chased? It was all different, all the same. The
question put to them: What do you want to be? Not, why*

*or who do you want to be, but a what, never with the Why.
The Why he always tried to ignore himself, for personal
reasons, and maybe, he thought, it was the same for all of
them. Maybe there is no Why.*

*There was a time when people died for what they
wanted to be. Now they just killed themselves. And that's
the maddening schism. The revealing crack. A time when
people fought to do what had to be done. Now they were
left with the vast choices laid out in front, dilettantes
wanting a bit of this, a piece of that, never deciding what
is worthwhile but always moving on to other trivial pur-
suits. Stick to one thing, he was told. One thing, and do
that well. Do it better than anyone else that came before.
And if you can't, then at least try. But don't fail before
you start.*

*And the question kept on at him. And the question
was too much to fill every day. And it was easier to relax
it all a little. Just let it chew itself. The body, the mind,
the wishes and the appetite. They weren't all characters,
they couldn't be. Like in some tidy airport fiction, where
all names and gaudy description have a set purpose. We
had the question in us, and with it so easy to ignore, why
wouldn't we?*

We all gathered together, the subterraneans pitted
against the over-ground men. Standing against the sky.
Laing had it right when he called it adjustment. It's not

an illness. They don't know anything.

As I walked I looked at the white as it turned to blue as it turned to dusk as it turned to black. I wondered at the stars, how much better they were for entertainment, how much more revealing than those dropped in the box. What my eyes saw shaped and gave meaning to all of the dark. I breathed in and out and it was gone again. Nothing stayed. I passed under the night sky. Nothing to believe in, not even the words I spoke or words I wrote: easy and inoffensive. And the breath I shot, it just washed everything with itself. Even as I spoke I lost interest, but that was key, to believe what you're saying and stick to it if questioned at a later date. I moved toward the edge of the bridge. I wasn't paranoid. Or schizophrenic. I knew what was going on. What was schizophrenia anyway, a broken heart, broken mind, merely adjusting to the scaffold already structured and built on foundations left behind? I looked down into the black river flowing. A web creeping through. Spun by spiders in clean spaces.

He had crossed the bridge now, headed around the corner. He breathed again, the anxiety had passed, but he kept watch. He wondered why eyes watched him go past. They must have known he was keeping one on them. How difficult it was for him to ignore them. It was close to obsession. Was it healthier to ignore them now? His activities were going too far. He sat with his knees in front of his face, like some unwashed child. Huddled on a bench

along the bridge. He thought if he could just sit there un-
til the contours peeled back and swept in the sick bodies,
and his own, he wouldn't have to wallow on stone lit by
numbing neon. He could swallow it all down without a
gasp, wrench it out and strangle the air with a shout that
went scratch.

And that would be it, he could settle as dust. Easy as
it was to form concepts and notions whilst sitting there,
formulating belief systems and ideas, he knew how dif-
ficult it was to put those opinions into life.

With no fear. No pain.

For all time.

And watch it all glow.

(INT.)

The seats were taken early in the park where people
lay. Benches exchanged under the shifting sunlight. Old
and young surveyed favoured spots and chose to take
them or not. If a potential neighbour was of an unfavour-
able cloth, they moved on and went silently elsewhere.

I take the seat under the heavy oak, away from the
sunlight, away from the playful and talkative. Anony-
mous waves.

In the corner of a dark vision, the shoes, the suede,
move toward and rest down the ankles and the socks and
the dangled leg. There is a rustling. Bread is ripped and
dropped. The pigeons creep over, swarming something

gentle through the air. The moving of bone. The Old Man mumbles crippled laughter through the well-kept goatee of gray and black. The crumbs flow down from the hand to the ground.

More birds today.

Now engaged, I must answer: More than usual.

Of course. They come for my breakfast. A clean smile.

A chuckle. A laugh held in, hidden behind the lips. They always come. Even the animals keep a schedule.

But they don't mind where it comes from.

True. They don't mind. I don't mind.

We watch over-fed wings make large movements for the bread. What's left of it. The man takes a bite then brushes off crumbs to the slabs beneath.

How are you today?

Today? Same as ever.

Same as ever.

And yourself?

Content. Satisfied. A breakfast for me. A breakfast for them. Keeps the ball rolling.

Certainly does.

What do you do around here?

I live. I exist.

And that's all?

I work.

Where do you work?

I point to my head.

I see. He takes another bite and talks out through each chew of every bite. *Yeah, yeah.*

And what about you?

What about me?

What do you do around here?

This. That. You know.

I suppose I do.

I'm a shipbuilder. That's my trade. Was my trade, I should say.

Not a lot of water around here.

You're right. He brushes more crumbs to the ground. A sparrow, orange in body and miniscule in stature darts in from the side, then freezes, and for a moment looks stuffed.

Ho-ho, a newcomer.

The larger pigeons ignore the miniature distraction. They peck at the ground, sometimes striking, sometimes picking up pieces too heavy for swallowing.

A group of youths brush by dragging their heels through stifled chatter. The young sparrow picks the remainders of what's left, hopping deftly on its small forked feet between the presence of gray. Before the desperate pigeons have time to angle their beaks at the thing, it flies off with its prize and stores it in some secret location, to rot or to be fed to some other.

All finished. He rises to his feet letting the crumbs fall knowingly. The winged creatures form a barrier a safe *distance from his now-swinging feet. Watching with a careful intensity. What remains is all they can have from him today.*

They pecked at the same small nothings and wanted it all for themselves, alone. One of the heavier set birds digging into the neck of its competitor. This was its adaptation.

Bye. I said.

The pigeons quarrelled in silence. A grounded fight of gray.

(EXT. KITCHEN - DAY)

When he arrived at the building, he entered through the back door, through the hallway. Post boxes. Names. He made his way up. Throat dry. He coughed and moved.

Watching the plughole haemorrhage, he poured away the stale liquid from the glass, to refill it from the tap. Cold. The water overflowed and trickled over the grip of fingers. He watched. The sound of the gushing water unreal, as if captured on film and recorded through a microphone. A soundtrack to his life that he now imagined. The notion a poison of the modern age.

He sat, as quietly as he could, smoking behind his window. He had lit the cigarette in haste, just get the

Thing rolling. He stared, letting the light dissipate from his vision, trying to turn his eyes off, as if in some meditative trance. The black crept in from all corners until each side made contact and the whole field of vision evaporated. He smoked the thing down to his fingers within seconds. He didn't feel the moments pass, but measured them by each pull he took on the smoke. That was his clock. Calculating further each cloud that exited his lungs, his diminished chest.

He felt like this was all that he could be.

He looked down at his arm, focussing and un-focussing on the forearm, his eyes a lens. Semi-automatic. He turned his arm, admiring the form, and thought to stub the ember slowly into the fleshiest chunk up near the joint, pushing the glowing red tip in deeper as the skin dried and edged away from the burn as it died.

He would feel nothing, watch the ash fly away and the tissue singing, recovering itself as best it could.

Can you smell that?

Yeah, smells nice.

Concealed, waiting for them to look up the wall, through the glass, he sat. They were close. So close he thought they would surely detect his observing eye. Then the tables would be turned on him. The reporter to be the reported. Words bellowed up inside his blackened lungs through to his head, waiting to say them if they peered up. He could see himself as if through ice, as if on a screen. His dreams had been overtaken by the feeling he was merely a viewer, watching him, watching film. All of it put back in the distance, void of him. And he was the actor. His head shook with apprehensive fear. What do you want? The gnashing teeth kept on through his mind.

What you looking at, he might say again, more threatening. Eyes bleeding a death black. Dark feeling in the chest. He didn't want to invite any violence up the wall but the feeling of dread was burning inside him. He wished himself away from this place.

Sounds of the road continued to brush along the pavement. The crunch of boots in gravel. He waited for the sweepers to pass. Wanting to make his speech to them but also wanting to not disturb the rest of himself and the street. And so he waited. They kept sweeping. Talking about someone or other that they knew, someone that had some problem, a problem easily solved to them it seemed.

I'm gonna report him tonight soon as I'm done.

Yeah. That'll calm him down.

Teach him a lesson won't it.

Yeah shit him up a bit.

Won't be doing that no more.

Yeah.

Their voices trailed off, but the sweeping remained close. He took a sip of tap water with the pill and waited, setting the glass back down on the floor slowly, silently. The glass connected on the boards with a dull thud that made him grit his teeth. All at once unaffected and affected. And then Nothing. He looked around to his left, the swinging trees waved at the grass. They whistled back. He looked at the glass and his empty packet of cigarettes. American cigarettes.

He stood there for a long time while the confused drum kicked in.

(INT.)

Sitting upright he picked up his pen and watched the road through the windshield, fuelled machinery fighting the open ground, beating it beneath. Confusing surroundings. Uniform streams of blackened engines and stable lines of cars swallowing up tarmac. He watched the car ahead and felt the parallel motions made in the stream. Two car lengths directly behind, expecting each jolt and bounce. The greens and reds. A billboard. On it stood a woman in a cage. The car behind continuing the same chain of thought along the stretch of road. And then another one back, then another and so on. He looked on, eyes level. Vehicles attached by some invisible connection viewed ahead like on some Hollywood dolly track. An empty plastic bottle. Engrained with some recognisable brand tumbling out of a truck cab up ahead. It bounced and whipped over the beaten road. His eyes blinked. The foreign body sensation. This sight, this lonely bottle cast upon the thundered highway, never to be revisited. Let's do this pure, he said, reaching into the right pocket. Let's do this real. Right. He said. Pulling a crumpled note from the stitched fabric.

He nodded his head forward, urging the vehicle, the driver, the old flesh and the metal. Accelerate. Like something telepathically communicated, the coughing driver pressed the metal. A string of words that empowers action, fuelling some eagerness to rapidly increase velocity. He imagined the scene in front of him, as if in memory. A day forgotten or remembered. He could not be sure which it would be. The grumbling engine drowned all the spoken words. He unravelled the note and reached an arm out the window. His arm hung close to the car adjacent. An offering for the road. An offering for the self. The parallel driver paid no notice. He focused mechanically on the action ahead, unsuspecting of the good fortunes he might snatch if only he relaxed the sockets and the fists. As words were shot to the mysterious breeze he released the note onto dusk's highway. Then the next. And the next. Until paper flipped and spun along the stretch behind. Yelps and stifled laughter came from their companion in the back seat. They turned back and watched. They saw drivers astonished. Their driver looked on with only a be-

mused expression. He pulled the rest out of his pocket,
the notes, the punched train and stamped bus tickets, the
plane tickets, the wallet, the coin, a pen, some card and
paper. They too were unleashed to the increasing winds.

The flutter. Reward enough. They don't look back but
instead hear some distant hooting and think, for a mo-
ment, it's following them. A siren.

Just drop me off here, he said.

Sure. The driver pulled the car over and the door
clicked. Unlocked.

Thanks.

He began to run.

(EXT. SKY - NIGHT)

The words dripped. I scratched through them. And
the clouds dreamed.

(INT.)

The darkness of vision snapped in an instant. Meditative state impossible. Too much noise. Too much distraction.

Wait until later.

Can never turn the eyes off. Open even when closed.
And never alone.

Pigeons surrounding my feet. Traces of a loaf already
falling.

Good morning.

Morning.

Didn't want to wake you. You seemed concentrated on something.

It was nothing.

More of them today.

If you keep coming so will they.

We'll see about that.

A tear. A flutter of long fingers dealing out the morsels of crusted bread. They fell heavier than their mass seemed to allow. Bouncing up off the ground. Then resting at the pink feet. They cooed their appreciation. Their desperation. The sparrows return. Yet this time a consensus had been reached. Move in on the outsider. Exile it. Get it away. They began their pecking. Their aggressiveness a useful survival instinct for now. But the sparrow too was quick. The orange puff swept about and avoided the thrusting eyes and sharpened beaks.

CHAPTER THREE

(EXT. STREET - NIGHT)

I walked home with the stink on me, my tongue loping around the gums of my mouth, soaking the stale tobacco and tasting the burning of the day. My hands searched my bones again. Something sharp. She had forgotten to take my key. So maybe I had left. I still didn't know. I thought to my Self that it didn't matter. It's what I tell my Self.

(INT.)

I walked up the stairs, one foot over the other, stumbling upward. I thought I heard a yelp as I approached the door. A screech. Nails on glass.

The neighbours were constantly fighting. Either fighting or spluttering up crusted lungs. You can hear it all through Styrofoam walls.

Televisions, milk cartons,
the circus leaving town
plastic and porcelain
life left in bed, or hurled into walls.
And never any laughter.

CUT TO: Laughter.

She wasn't there when I got in. The door swung as I listened for any sign of movement. Any sign of life. I left the key on the table next to the telephone. I helped my self to some of her cigarettes. The whole carton still full but one. Putting a few in different pockets. Setting my self up for a pleasant surprise for whenever I ran out. I took another packet, left the carton empty, wondered why she didn't take some if she was leaving.

He wore a bemused expression. Strange, he said. Strange.

I put one behind my ear and I took off my clothes. I listened to the fabrics crawl off my skin and enjoyed the ringing silence that followed. I stood there with every-thing hanging out, nauseating and strangling to hold on, and lit her cigarette.

I moved through all the right doors to get to the bathroom and twisted the squeaking bath tap. After a while: Hot. I left the water running, allowing the steam to rise up the tiles unobstructed. I thought I should have a quick peak, see that she definitely wasn't around. I didn't want my last hot bath interrupted by all the teeth she would rattle at me.

The door lurched as I opened it and it was cold be-ing that naked, so I only poked my head into each room. She seemed to have made a swift exit herself: her leath-er suitcase gone. The wardrobe doors splayed open, emptied out, bras and underwear lying about the floor, hanging on the bed. The way things might look if a room gets turned upside down by crack-fiending thieves. The cartons were all full of smokes and I smiled. I stacked them up in a pile and left them by the door. In the bathroom, the bottles all emptied of chalks. I felt something inside me gnawing ticklish.

I shrugged, pretending not to care. As if someone was watching. I even looked around, for multiple camera angles, and repeated the action. I tried to shake off the pain and tapped the ash of the quick burning cigarette out onto the carpet. I noticed none of the books were gone. I thought I could stash a couple, maybe sell them. I'd have to find the good ones though. Stolen first editions. Would take time, and patience, as we'd developed a habit of always planting books in unexpected places, never stacking them alongside each other like some chained down bookstore. But the flat was small, I could cover it and all its nooks and hiding places in an hour tops.

I spotted Fante under the sink. We left the books to breathe and live on their own, like those people who call words and pages their friends, visiting upon them like old acquaintances whenever we came across one. In a cupboard, under the bed, behind the wardrobe or in our heads. All our friends lived there. How quaint. History was the distillation of the one that acted, against those who didn't. Reading the greats, what of the thousands, the millions in slumber who weren't. Were they not worthy of mention?

I spotted another as I went back into the bathroom. *Island* lay with the toilet paper.

(INT.)

Tragic consequences are only tragic because they're looked at as such. And really for no other reason than a signal of the laze taking hold. An easy temptation to blame it on something. Does this mean something? To scapegoat the feelings and put them down to some external force. In some darkened corner. Owing it all to random consequence, that's resolving of responsibility. Not only dangerous and lazy, but also limiting. Another fetter of the free mind. Sometimes lying down, she would tuck herself up and imagine, visualise her deathbed, contemplating all that led to those creeping final moments. She'd guess how many beats her heart could make, between now and then, counting each one that kept her conscious. Blinking and perceiving.

She pictured the bed dripping brown-yellows, jaundiced and rotting. Her body sinking more assuredly in, accepting the final purge and releasing the ears back to the standing roots—momentarily whispering to the wind—and then falling in grace. What about the child her eyes would ask. The child.

She thinks of the next meal and how they could all

be the one: the last one. She became gradually more aware, more obsessed with these thoughts, slowly more comfortable with the outcome. End the banging drum and end it with finality. Into unrelenting depths. Preferably, she thought, the sensation of drowning. Perhaps that would be an appropriately painful ebb, dessert for the wild unfettered hedonism and Dionysian crime that had co-existed with her other half. Unrelenting, valueless, disgusting. Preparing the nest. Decorating the grave. Picking the plot. Dropping the flowers.

This all saddened her. She looked at people differently. She looked at them with a powerful lucidity. She seemed to know what was to be now. People were ageless at the same time as wearing the strangling cobwebs of time. When she listened she looked right into the face, the eyes. Attentively taking notes. She could see them as young, as old, as they were and as they might have been, as if making a list of struggles to solve and administer in the Next place. She didn't believe in a Next place. Their faces melted and expanded with her imagination. She pictured white. Piercing white. Darkness beneath. What it would be like closing her eyes. Getting some feeling of coming down the mountain.

She wondered if she were fed to the pigs, how they would nourish every joint and bone and chunk of flesh. How all hope would be gone in paperwork. How it would all be gone. Back into the universe: free. Her cells transformed. This confused them both.

(EXT. BATHROOM - DAY)

I rose up onto the side of the bath and kept the screams down inside as the tips of my toes entered the steaming water. Then the leg and the abdomen and the warming solar plexus. I lowered. Gently. I sat, then lay back. I began to think: it was a fragility of mind. I adapted my self to certain things immediately. Always accepting things as they were. And now I began to see this as a weakness. I never fought against the things that I saw, what I thought were the injustices. I never rallied for a cause. I only got used to those fatalistic death shots calling. I never wanted to be a tiresome teller of stories. I only wanted to express my self in my way. Not tell the tale of some other man in some other place or some other time.

Stuck here in dripping time, the burning of the bath brought back a tunnel of memory and I thought of when we first met, the protest, and how I had so eagerly adapted then:

👁

(INT.)

Droning insentient thousands had been gathering there, through word of mouth and by the abject power of mass telecommunication. They now marched heads-up through the once-buzzing banking district. Now the tall monuments of ice stood desolate and hummed not with glory or the transient feeling of success, but with a misery that permeated the entire city. Metro Polis lined the road. Standing behind improvised metal barriers with whistles and batons in hand, riot gear cloaking their bodies and faces from any recognition or attack. The day brought the promise of ironing out some of the undesirables. The chance to crack the skull of the Dangerous Class. Spill the brains. Plunge a fist into an already shattered cranium. The Metro Polis were the protectors of what was already a baneful society sick with the fear and in constant reform toward disaster and against its own people, against civilisation. And against any notion of enlightenment. The news screens dotted on walls in offices, newsstands and coffee houses showed them moving toward the meeting point. Humble figures all of the same ominous ilk. Masked, blacked out eyes, angry young hoodlums or focused provocateurs. An image so distant from the reality of actual discontent, which in actuality was more like masses of spectacle-wearing middle classes, that even setting out on the march they felt justified. Egged on by the teasing news corporations. They felt an affirming reassurance at being so closely knitted together. One set of enemies on one side and another set of enemies on the inside. But today they would not be competing as they did in the working hours, forcefully setting one family against another. They would unlock possibility. Today their brains connected on a frequency that resonated with the other. They were there for the same reason and their minds pulsated with mutual understanding. The same was true with the militarised music in the ears of the Metro Polis. The rhythm bringing with it ideas, memories. Known functions. Repeaters. Like shotguns. And it echoed the truth. That the twenty percent of somnambulists in any given population watched them both with a fear? Or was it admiration? It was surely neither; they were watched with disgust by the news-chomping twenties, the ones fed so easily and happily by the Metropolis newswire and the O Press and the rest of them.

What if the common frequencies could be shifted toward a more agreeable pitch? Agreeable to whom? Without the communicators under their shirtsleeves it would be a discordant impossibility. The electricity of the mind had to be harnessed before that of the earth. It began with understanding. What use was this mass of communication to the everyday man if it was put to the use they saw that day. The old adage of dividing and conquering. Surely this was useless to mankind in its present state. But it was useful to those wanting to ignore, wanting to sell something. News was like Burroughs' heroin. The user was sold to it, not the product sold to the user. They thought they were benefiting from the onset of electrical means flowing through the everyman on every day. But what was really gained? Distraction from thought. Distraction from freedom. Convergence toward uniformity and conformity. But what was conformity if one didn't believe in the concept? Conformity was set up through and by the mass communicators. There was no avoiding it. The message was clear: Conformity means direction. And it was the same as ever, but that doesn't mean the common goal is a good one. But if you can guide the people into understanding differently, then there's a hope for salvation. But not for the ones at the bottom of the pyramid. Was it conspiracy? Of course not, that was the easy answer. It was simply good business. Sound and strong. And it was their greatest goal in fashioning solid managers out of the buried and the lost. Reliable managers for a system without questions or questioners. In answer to a question never posed. They *do* think it's funny, turning rebellion into money. And what good did it do him to ask these questions? If he simply went along with them, life would become easy, smooth. He would be respectable. If he had that, then maybe he would have happiness. The temptations never ceased.

(EXT. CITY STREET - DAY)

The marchers piled on through the derelict streets accompanied by their armoured escort, both itching for a fight but only one half of them armed for it. Every now and then a rumbling came from outside the procession, a baton flashing through constricted vision into the body of some quivering protestor. Volatile authorities circled in choppers above; journalists were sure to stay on the outside of the marching boundaries, but through repeating the citizen's footage back they could make out as if they were amongst it. Rather than merely on the outskirts of reason. They were fighting for justice too, but it was the reverse. They were just spectators, refusing to get too close.

He was stuck in the middle, the sounds of the polis and the people mingling into a crescendo of noise that jarred his innards. Their bellies roared for revolution, a revolution that would end the oligarchy, create social conditions capable of change. Their dissatisfaction bubbled through each and every set of shuddering entrails screaming for an end to economical barbarism. But it was misplaced, they wanted to replace one domination with another, seeing to it that there was an end to the metal rain of authority only to be replaced with a new bureaucracy, something they chose not to foresee.

Symbiotic or separate. Forgotten, broken. And it was peaceful, non-violent, it should be said.

That was at least until they arrived on the final stretch.

We settled in and gathered around, planting ourselves defiantly on the ground, as one by one a crop of ringleaders took turns in directing the ears of our home-made circus. They were the self-importants. The ones that did it for the status. They did it for the moral superiority they thought came with it. I don't think it ever occurred to them they were just as puerile as the last man. Nietzsche's last man. But the feeling of self-confidence, even arrogance, that oozed from them was nonetheless contagious. What would it be like having a piece of that? The answer came with the first: a member of this young anti-capitalist party, from this university that everybody had heard of but no one had gone to. He settled everyone down with his high-pitched whistle that he blew louder and longer, directly into the ears of us closely surrounding him. We quietened down, turning to look him in the face as he stepped up onto a blue milk crate he carried in his black-gloved hands. We gave him his moment in the rain.

He urged us to silence, gesturing with his arms and waiting patiently for the last blood-screams of die fascist scum die to wretch out of a last man's mouth before he began his personal rally. His curly hair spread across to the side of his face from sweat after small, calculated scuffles with the authorities. He mopped his brow with his glove, taking it off as he began to shout to the gathered, speaking out to us as if he was some beat poet: My name is Breker and I want to tell you something. The hallucination of truth that we believed in, the suggestibility of our society, touched by the far-reaching technology of the modern age, is being witnessed here all around us today. But it is dying. The spectators on one side believe one thing, (he pointed across to the side where tourists snapped digital photographs) and the protestors here on the inside believe another thing (he opened his arms as if to embrace us). The kettle is beginning to steam. The rain beginning to fall. The onslaught of developing technology has never been questioned, but we must put our backs up to the machinery and ask: are these advances good for us, for mankind, good for the average human?

He cleared his throat.

They never thought to consider what was happening, just as long as we slide across the cash and the cut plastic. Gaining in confidence, his arm reached out and spread over the crowd.

And they put it to us like a fist inserted in the mouth. He formed the fist. The constant slow death of the inner man that held each of us down, the refusal to denounce the flag, the state, the government, and announce our freedom, putting us out of reach, out of contact.

Make no mistake (the fist raised high). We are not Luddites.

Education is *our* answer. I started to think maybe he had a point.

But even when the government gives it to us, for those god-awful years of New Terror, nothing changes.

In fact it gets worse. Much worse. (His throat began to scrape from his shouting. He held on clenching his fist trying to keep his voice loud above the restless crowd).

The technology on the outside provides too much distraction, an easy door that leads to some kingdom of the mind untouchable by any education or learning.

They offered us new tools: It'll make your life easier.

It'll change your life.

It'll change the way you live.

Your life will never be the same again.

And they offer us add-ons and plug-ins and applications and peripherals and downloads and Easter eggs and updates until we don't know what to do with our selves any more apart from clamber for it. (He began to go off on a tangent, as if he had harboured some concealed but longstanding hatred for these things.) And all the while the super-rich get richer and the poor simply die. (He returned to the tried and tested material.)

But we sat cosily insulated from the world, insulated from reality, hidden and cushioned from the real problem.

And so our minds began to eat themselves and each other.

He stood down trailing off on his last words.

Some cheered, they nodded Yes, of course, as if to say there could be no discussion of this obvious truth, without analysis, just acceptance. Some just wanted to be on the inside, with some secret knowledge, but in the end it was for the purpose of making themselves feel exceptional. At the root of all of the rhetoric there were hidden motives kept unspoken. And just as every man deludes himself constantly, they thought that they might be immune from this labyrinth of denial. But they weren't. None of us were.

They were glad, some of them, to be on the unpopular side, to be going against the wave, for the thrill of it or for the feeling that they were somehow better. Superiority rather than kinship. It was good to have something to complain about, they seemed to think. It took the pressure off. And it was the gift that the middle class wanted to give to the poor. But the poor didn't care. They were already too ritually obsessed with riches. And the middle classes deluded themselves too, that they weren't obsessed with the power or the freedom for instruction that came with money. Silent columns that tower over mere men, pillars that crumble and favour ethereal time. They thought they couldn't be polluted by it. They were pure and for the people. Not for the self. Only some were forever trapped.

As the poor geared up for another night in the pub, a cache of pills in the club and a wrap of powder up the snub, the middlers blurted impotent slogans and shouted for the freedom of the people. They walked among the forest of cathedrals and churches, remnants of dust and fabric masked everywhere. But the people didn't seem to notice or want to notice. The activists were hippies, crazies, as they had been taught. They didn't have real problems. So apathy was handed out like bread to the hungry and it filled the stomachs. Sometimes satisfied. Here take this, all of you. And eat it. This is your body. Given up, for me.

Alive and peaceful. The impoverished wanted escape, complete transcendence from the bitter melancholy that translated into complete bliss and enslavement to the machinery. Little engines powering the shit box. The working class that participated at the march wore uniforms and carried weapons. They had titles and masks. They had numbers on their shoulders they removed before the ruckus ensued. They would soon take much joy in the violence. But later they might have wished they were there independently. They would wish they had turned up with harder weapons.

A small surprise had been planned.

The Old Man withdrew from the gang of press on the perimeters of the march, and as the camera shutters went with all flashbulbs popping, he entered the revolving door. He made his way up the stairway. He knew she would be waiting. The door was locked. He knocked. She turned the key.

Hello.

Greetings.

I see you have the bag.

Of course.

Let them have what they want.

Walking over to the window, the crowd amassed below. The glass buildings reflected the sun down into their eyes. The view of them seemed to him like a colony of ants, but he ignored the obviousness of this observation. He started throwing out the notes a handful at a time until the bag got empty enough and he could flip it under and shake out all the paper. Teeming insects all of them together rustling under the dried leaves. He saw them as people. The King's head flipped and spun as it caught the breeze. He watched it tumbling, she behind him watching the door for broken entries. He mumbled laughter to himself as he saw the first ones reaching out their hands and clutching.

Back down on the ground Breker continued his speech. He stepped back onto his homemade podium: We will *not* stand *idly* by while the innocent are raped and pillaged. We will not work ourselves so deep into the ground and into the machine that...

A five note slipped itself onto his cheek. He swiped at it with his glove. He stared at it. Always his head down on the note, he wiped the sweat again, slowly comprehending what he had caught in his open mouth.

The notes kept tumbling down, the crowd cut silent and watched for a moment as the paper drifted in the breeze. A scream from the back. A woman in disbelief:

It's cash it's cash.

The mass slowly began to jump, arms innocently outstretched, not trusting their eyes, not believing the fortune being squandered and not understanding. Their lives shrunk down to the concentrated moment. The Now.

They leapt and grabbed at the air, using bodies as ladders, jumping over each other and trampling backs and hands and arms and faces with their feet. They pardoned and smiled. It was new. The slow frenzy had begun and the Old Man tumbled out more notes: a fresh black sack of tens. He threw them out in a haste, pausing for a moment to watch, then grabbing the next sack. He emptied the twenties. The scene was more paper than people as they hurried around pushing and barging toward the drop zone.

It's happening.

Of course it is, she said.

The Polis now looked up and the journalists, not knowing whether to grab or to herd control, reached out their arms. Waves of truncheons beat down on the crowd, as if they had been given an excuse to pound blissful violence into the dispersed rioters.

FUCKING GRAB IT people yelled FUCKING GET IT.

The swelling swept in and surrounded, like thumping feet on porcelain tiles. A release as forgiving as it was forsaken. Rubber treads beating for blood.

The Old Man picked up the last two sacks and held onto them tight at the window ledge.

You should watch this, he said, looking at them like people.

I've seen it before.

He turned out the bags, watching down on the eager faces pelting about and looking up still not noticing the source of the cash flow. OI YOU. He hummed a tune to himself as he dropped out the first sack, the whole thing. Full of fifties. Two spotted it immediately on its plummet past the building and before it struck the young man on the head, the bag had been seized and then ripped to shreds between the two hands. FUCKING MOVE. Breker held it from one end as a faceless Metro Polisman yanked at it, stretching it from the other. Their survival instincts kicking in. The horses sent wild. In their eyes they recognised themselves. The man in black began to swing his staff at Breker as he held on, ducking his head to protect himself from the blows. He struck at the fingers holding on, turning red beneath the gloves as they were beaten into shattered submission. Yet Breker refused to let go. His fingers were smashed into useless dangling flesh inside his gloves. He fell to the ground, more Metro Polis running in with kicks and fresh rubber treads. Beating at his face with fists and weapons alike.

He still held on. The Old Man watched from above. He knew this would happen. They both did. The Metro Polis-man pulled the sack out of the mash of fingers and held it aloft signalling victory to his comrades. There was a small cheer audible amongst the roars of voices going hoarse from quick opportunism. Bodies lay almost still, strewn in a mess as livelier ones bounded over them to pick up the loose and still-falling bills scattering on the pavement. The young man lay next to Breker, both knocked out temporarily. The Old Man briefly looked down at them both and saw dead ants.

I shook it off and rose to my feet, looking back at Breker then glancing upward to see the last sack emptied. The pinks flitted in the sunlight as they fell gently through the air. The limp bodies were piling along the road as the animals ran at the spot where the notes hung in the air. They fell slowly, tantalising, yearning to be had, white wisps cut from the field.

I stood up as I saw the last confrontation. Polis versus Polis, man against woman against man. Punches were thrown. Kicks came in. Someone dived over the pile. They knocked their heads together as they reached for the prize. Hands massacred themselves for the cash, receiving violent stamps from heavy feet. The women were left crying in the street as the men took the fight to each other. With handfuls of cash in one hand and clenches of paper in the other, they beat each other for the glory of it, forgetting the notes. The rioters swarmed in on the forces, the cloaks and the horses hysterical not knowing what to do apart from click into war mode. The electronic devices, now useless, were used as armour and as weapons, holding up radios and breaking them on bones in the onslaught. Red and black caved on the heads, not crying out but still reaching for the chance. Panic and striking distance meeting in the sight of the thick forest.

Unknown to them then, we would later hear that a severe blow to the head, from a Metro Polis radio, had killed a man. His name was Hari Kelvin.

Before that day he was anonymous, but after it, his name would become synonymous with the rise of the political Metro Polis. Hari lay crumpled next to the barriers as the elderly and the young collapsed at his feet. He bled from the eye in a stream coming down and out to his ear. The thin hair caked on his forehead as the blood dried, as the day dried and as the tears loomed in the forms of flesh flattened beside his. The sadness and the death rolled together into the storm drain.

She stood still, ready for the crash of uniform through the locked door. But it never came. The Old Man turned to her and said: Let's go. She nodded, so they unlocked the door again and cautiously moved down the hallway. It was silent, the soundproof windows doing their job.

They went down the stairway, not risking the lifts for an inopportune meeting of force and helmet. They kept on down, going past the white halls and the offices until they came out the turning doors.

When they exited the young man stood there smoking a cigarette nervously. I looked, shaking my head. They had a cold furious look in their eyes. They picked up their legs and fled. I followed.

Where are you going. Come back here.

They didn't turn back. They kept moving on.

Hey COME BACK HERE!

They chased through the pamphleteered streets and down past all the barriers, the metal and the march moving away from them in the background. They kept running, first down the main road then down a side street. The Polis moved up the main street behind them in a flurry of dogs and horses and marching shields, batons and delight. They would get their fight. Their radios no longer operational. Communication breaking down. One was already dead. They ran in unison, the clunk of their armour on their backs, the war faces sprinting toward the scene. It was justified. There would be no repercussions for this. They laughed and jeered and pushed hard at each other, jostling to get there first.

The fugitives moved on through the alleys and kept on going. They dropped the evidence behind in a black bin, never stopping, getting rid of anything that might identify them. She removed her black hood and pulled it off, revealing a white top underneath as she jogged, slowing down to throw the jumper in the next bin. The Old Man had unusual stamina. He kept it going too, he ran at a steady pace and couldn't be stopped. The young man heaved as the lungs began to give way.

COME back he wheezed. Come BACK.

Just want to

talk.

They glanced back with a look coquettish, especially her. It kept him following. He rubbed his head where the bag had struck him and kept on at it. They belted through the parades, somehow gaining pace. They ran through outdoor café tables, mingled people and chairs and chirpy voices with their heads down. Their lips were smiles.

Come on, her eyes seemed to say. Don't give up.

They had been running for what seemed like a night. The light was giving way and they moved toward a red sunset. It wasn't dark yet. He saw the Old Man fall back to a jog and then a walk. I was far back. Still about 150 meters along the long road. She stopped too and went back for him, jostling his arm in encouragement. She said something.

Wait.

Come on wait.

I coughed and spluttered out something useless and kept going now at a loose run, the limbs all flaccid and falling around me, dangling off the joints. Keep on coming: the eyes.

They stood in the street and waited for him.

You're not going to give up, are you? The Old Man said as he approached.

No I just want to talk.

Well what is it, what are you officer? What are you? You look like plain clothes.

No. I'm not.

He looked at her as if for support, she looked to the Old Man.

Let's take him with us. He might have a place we can stay.

I paused, thinking it over. They weren't dangerous, from what I could see. Mischievous maybe. I considered it, already knowing what I would answer. I had a rule not to refuse anyone back then. Just play it out, without saying sorry to the dice game.

Ok. Come with me.

She smiled, a small one, and the Old Man sighed as he followed.

What's your name?

Don't worry about that, what's yours?

Arthur Sonntag I said without taking a breath, have you got a cigarette?

Yeah.

She reached into the back pocket of her jeans and produced some roll-ups all tightly packed into a used box of Davidoffs.

Thanks. He took it. She lit it for him seeing him first reach into the pockets left and right for his lighter.

Where do you live, Arthur?

Just up here, it'll be another 15 minutes walk. Five if we sprint.

Okay, she looked back to the Old Man and paused for him, not watching to avoid making him feel his age.

You alright? I asked him.

Yeah fine just keep moving. Come on. Where is it?

Just up here. I pointed.

We tracked up the street a little further, a few more words, where is this going? I kept looking at her, how she moved, slinking through the street, smoking confidently and watching the ground ahead of her. She dipped off the pavement here and there and walked along the road. I watched her and she knew it. I thought that somehow she was used to being watched.

Right, I said, unnecessarily loud, as if to voice my anxiety that they may ransack the place at any moment. The voice of a landlord belting out of me needlessly. Sorry, right. It's up here.

We went up and I opened the door; a gust of muck

came out as we went in. They didn't seem to notice. I went over to the desk and hung my coat on the back of the chair before picking up another pack of cigarettes and showing her, Davidoffs. Do you want one?

Not right now, thank you. She smiled, a bigger smile this time. I felt impotent. Under the heat of those eyes.

She sat down, squeezing down slowly into the worn sofa.

A drink?

Sure.

I listened to them conversing in low tones as I walked to the kitchen. I grabbed three mugs and poured in some coffee. Some milk. SUGAR? I shouted.

No answer.

I went in and saw them, he smoked a long fine cigarette from a pearly-white holder and she, looking up at me, broke her sentence off.

Sugar? I said again, expectant, ingratiating and grating.

Well it depends what we're having, she said.

Coffee, sorry, yeah coffee, unless you want something else?

I had the inside feeling I'd become the host to a cosy little group of terrorists. I looked in on my self and wondered just how desperate I had become. I opened the curtains as I awaited an answer, attempting to make the place presentable by shining some light on the situation.

The sky hung in a dark red.

No. Thank you. I only have sugar with tea.

Ok, sure. I went to walk out of the room.

I'm fine too, the Old Man said with a quiet smirk. I paused.

Yes sorry, would you like something else, sorry what is your name?

Same as her. Don't worry about that yet.

I smiled, hospitable, pathetic and moved into the kitchen, then brought out the coffees. I usually took two sugars, but I left them out this time.

It's cold.

Oh, shit sorry. I'll put some on fresh. Sorry I didn't realise. I'm a bit. You know.

Don't worry. Just leave it. The Old Man said.

Right, I nodded. So. Are you going to tell me who you are? I don't usually have strangers in here. I've never befriended people in circumstances like that.

Haven't you?

No. I wondered what he meant. Puzzled expressions back and forth.

Well. What do you want us to tell you?

(INT.)

The words began to run faster, the thoughts and ideas

always there only until I actually sat down and tried to write them. Trying to translate my mind. They would be lucid at the point of conception, following one after the other, but only when I was outside and breathing the fresh air. Each line spoke itself in my mind. But then the words would all congeal and mould into an indecipherable cluster once I took the seat. It was no good.

I rested my head on a wet towel she had left behind. I watched the ceiling, and the vapour rising to it. I would go see Grandpa. The Old Man. It was time. I had waited four straight months for something to be returned: a manuscript, a poem, a rejection, anything. Like a long day drawn out across an entire lifetime, I felt as if my hours were swimming down to the ocean. The river stream lost. Money was spent. The jar was empty. Inspiration low.

He'd always treated me with respect that Old Man, and for that he was endeared to me. But for no other reason I could think of. He taught me to perceive, to breathe reality. But he was a pitiful old hermit. He had always stayed on the fringes, believing that to be some kind of answer. He was self-deprecating and compassionate in a way that was ingenuous, not like how most people self-deprecate, expecting compliments to the contrary. He really meant his words, with sourness, and rarely spoke ill of anyone. Anyone but the government. The self-serving institutions, as he numbered them. And of course, his old colleagues at the Newswire. The Last Men. He said he'd write a book about them. Maybe he had. I pondered that everything I had learnt, my entire existence, all required his input. That's what he told me. I needed him. He didn't say that. But I thought there was only one I needed. I refused to face that one, simply turned it off. I didn't think it possible before, to play the part-time nihilist, being able to switch human feeling off and ignore reality, but it was easy. And it helped me get through things, the times of nothingness and empty holes. It really did.

I'd have to get together anything I had to bring to the Old Man. I wouldn't turn up empty handed. Put a brave face on the horrors. Mask the reality. A mask for the mask for the mask.

As he watched the steam send its wispy clouds up, resigned and empty, he compared in his odious mind the thoughts that he had for some reason wanted to express. Even in the most oppressive times – in fact that was when it was strongest – the words lay across the imaginary page. Solemn and strong. But the meaninglessness, the pretension, subsisted as he pondered: Love is like the bath. Gathering all the meaning in one hand, the clouded and dark water dripping out in time with the metronome of his thoughts. The open door. If another were to enter, the tub would overflow and trickle out to the other rooms, eventually descending to the rooms below. The steam kept rising, until it reached the ceiling and rose no longer. A ghoul fanning out and disappearing. Until the bath grew cold. Until the other departed. Until the water sank back down through the open plughole and out into the pipes. Love was like his bath, he pondered. It was a lot like that.

But now he had written it out, scrawled it in ink to first see how the words stood, it had been bled of all significance. Life would enter his mind, an idea. Then he would translate it through weak expression onto the page. First thoughts on the curling edge of it. Then by the time it was read out, the voice or the head, it had died again. The page killed it. He thought it better to leave it in his head.

He needed a boost, some encouragement, but what good would that be anyway? The melancholy of his days seared him again, his vision tunnelling into sadness.

Life would never enlist him.

PART THREE

White

Iris Out

CHAPTER ONE

(EXT. BEDROOM - NIGHT)

My hands rested loose on my lap, hunched over I stared out the miserable window, my eyes feeling like the lids had been sliced off. Can't close them now. And the eyes, they're never rested. Even in dreams. And hers, never closed. They still stared out underneath those jelly eye-flaps. I blinked mine. It was pale blue skies and bright eyes out there, so I kept the window shut, kept it out. Shuddered the curtains across some more. Looking at my coffee, my arm reached forward to lift the sad thing up to my mouth. Some pages, 13,579 words. Was it like this for the others? Whole sentences, entire constructions, underlined by that fearful decay.

When I stood up there was a dull tingling down the whole of my left side. The leg, the foot, the arm, the abdomen. A headache, gripping to the left.

I know what I'm writing. I know. But I need to start fresh, to unlearn.

Unlearn.

CHAPTER TWO

He had been watching from the window intermittently for around four hours. All he could see were the distant closed blinds glowing something red. White. He tossed his cigarette from the window, watching it fall fast as it caught the weight of wind and rain. A small shadow, which he knew was just a plant, stood there motionless in the window across. He watched. The glowing dimmed and brightened. It flickered as the television changed channels. He could tell they were changing channels. The room went black then light, every other second, reaching hypnotic rhythm. The blinds dropped, but there, midway up, remained a crack in the folds. He thought they were onto him.

He had watched enough rooms to know when they were watching television and when they were changing channels, and when they sensed something. He had learned that much. His eyes didn't move as he sat there urging something to happen. Could he go across there and introduce himself? *Hi, I live across the way, just wanted to drop in and say Hello.* No, he couldn't do that. That would be a disturbance. And disturbing. He wanted them as they were, pure, untouched and without the knowledge of him there observing. He waited for some sign of activity that would keep him intrigued. Any movement. A ground floor shadow long and stretched walked past the window. He lurched forward a little closer to the glass and put his hand on the sill, his mouth opening a little, white sputum reaching from one lip down to the other. A steady exhale hummed out as he watched with his face almost touching the glass, the sputum vibrating like a string. The window steamed with the condensation of his breath. He wiped it impatiently. The branches outside waved, moving into his line of sight. Obscuring his vision. He repositioned and tilted his head to the side, improving the view. He swayed left to right in motion with the tree as he tried to keep a close eye on his subject. Condensation again.

The light went out. The television off, he thought. Was it even a television? Yes, it must be. He knew when it was a television and when it wasn't. He knew, he knew. There was a visible disappointment on his darkened face. He edged away from the window and tried to keep steady as he stepped away from the wooden chair. His diet of cigarettes and water leaving him feeble.

When he walked over to the only lit candle it quivered and sent the light flickering, forming a ripple of shadows behind him. He slowed as he approached the table and leant down to deliver a jet of air, extinguishing the flame. He stood by the table in the pitch darkness.

He used a candle to keep discreet, avoiding the electric light and, being so well practiced now, he didn't even need the bulb as a guide. Walking to the next room he sat on the thin mattress. It made a desperate noise as he sunk in. There was no other sound apart from the occasional car that rolled by on the street four floors below. Itching his arm he thought to himself, he wanted a cigarette. There were none left. He checked his pocket again, finding only a box of matches. He took the matches out and laid them on the table. He hadn't left his flat for two and a half weeks. His shoes sat in the corner with their black laces frayed, light brown muck drying on the soles. Smoking up all of his supplies and eating on a tight ration he had resolved to stay awake through the nights, drawing distractions from his view out of the window. Maybe he could go across, maybe they urged for some contact. Like him. But it wouldn't be real. It would be false and impure. It would be something outside of his and outside of their usual experience. It would be strange at first, yes, but then maybe they would become acquaintances. And then possibly friends. He could hoist them over when he felt the hands pulling him down, he could talk to them and listen to them and they could get along and everything would be better, the loose emptiness would be filled by something else and they would be better off for it. *He* would be better off for it. But how could he break through that first hurdle. And wouldn't one emptiness replace another? He thought back to the protest. How could he introduce himself without being deceptive and without breaking boundaries? He could tell them about his day, working at the Newswire, yes, Metropolis. They knew of it. He could tell them about the biting office politics and the one-upmanship and they would listen and they would care, sympathising because they couldn't understand their own problems, but they would understand his. He could listen to them and they would confide in him and he would nod and think and reach out and they would all feel something. It would all make sense.

He blinked hard. An old lady. Lifting the lid on the bin and peering in, analysing the contents. White carrier bags inside, filled to the stinking brim. She closed the lid quietly and shuddered off with her coat and her feet. He blinked hard, felt like a lizard.

He looked again, across the way, in a state of mild confusion. Now the room was empty. The television gone. No flickering. No blinds.

He searched for them, somewhat frantically, the white of his eye snapping to grid.

Then he saw them there, sat inside, as if nothing had happened, on the next floor up.

It would still be another three nights before Niall Samstag decided to face himself and leave the flat.

Contemplation of the fourth floor kept his mind busy as he looked for a way out.

His mind dwindling down the stairwell. He would soon come down from the mountain.

CHAPTER THREE

(INT.)

I walked in an instant. It all picked up and blurred around the squeaking leathers. They were confused, my shoes. The untied laces black and swinging. And my legs tumbled like each step was about to crumble, be the last, each step differently formed. Stumbling and false. My feet watched each part of the other and its respective leg, confused and looking up or down in mocking insult. The rest tried to straighten it out, do the walk, whatever that looked like. So I started running but that simply built a faster barrier of questions to hurdle. How do you, or I, run again? Just go faster. It will soon be over, it will be over in a minute. *Excuse me there, Father figure, how long is a minute?* That'd be sixty seconds. *How come sixty?* What do you mean? *And how long is a second?* Look, I don't believe in time, Son, but at your age, this is what they want you to learn. To be able to count, find answers, make dealings, not more questions like the ones you've got. *Erm, what would that be though, Father figure?* That's precisely it. *What is?* The truth, or the quest for it. *What does quest mean?* Precisely. *But I already have it.* Ha-ha. Well what is it? *It changes all the time.*

How often? *Quicker than a second, I think.* Millisecond, microsecond? Nano? *No, none of those, it just cuts up. It's Instant, like noodles. Like there was no time, to make it or beat it.* I see. Well, it agrees with my disregard for time. *So why not kill time.* If I don't acknowledge it, it's as good as killing it. *What about driving, moving, walking – don't you count how long they might take? Like to cook a chicken?* A hint, Son? *I could eat. Could always eat.* So if it appeared in front of you in an instant, what might you say? *I don't know... aren't we having pizza anyway?* Unfortunately, because Father figure disregards time, he also disregards a steady wage. You know what that is? *Time for money. Or money for time. But don't I want money? Why? To buy us all pizza.* Well, then that's alright, I suppose ... I want Time. Not money. *Can you have both, or only one at a time?* That's what we're all finding out... well, some. *Is that why Mother only has money?* She has both, for you, when it counts, for both of us. *It means a lot to Mama, doesn't it?* What's that? *Money.* Some sleep on their knees for it. *But not you?* Not me ... nor you ... yet. No. *I want to be like you Father figure.*

I don't know if you do.

CHAPTER FOUR

On the morning of the third day, he sat sipping the last specks of coffee remaining in the jar. He mixed in the hot water, stirred it with a gritted spoon and lifted it out of the mug to his lips, tasting the dirt water. He reflected with solemnity. His job: gone. He was unemployed for the first time since the age of twenty-one. The worry of dealing with petty practicalities sullied his countenance. Leaving work three weeks ago without a word, without recompense, not returning any calls, was a sure way to lose it all. Maybe they just thought he was dead. Run down on the way to the office. Stabbed in the supermarket. Locked in his bathroom. They'd believe it. Maybe. No. He was still unwilling to return to the office and find out. He couldn't face it.

He sighed as he looked in a drawer for something to smoke. What had been the purpose? It was all clear then, crystal, *as an azure sky of deepest summer*. His hands brushed over the kitchen counter; he knew there was nothing. He had never been bullied, had an easy life, no illness, no tragedy, no affecting deaths in the family, no lashings, no beatings from his father, enough food on the table, enough light in the house. On the surface of it, all that he needed. Where had the urge presented itself? At what point had the decay set in? Where was the rot taking hold? He looked in another drawer, finding matches, a torch, nothing of any use. Maybe he could sell his things to pay the rent. He refused to be left out on the street. It was no place for him. How did such a lucky man come down with such impotent rage, against the world, against his life, against himself? He checked another cabinet, moving the few items of crockery on the shelf. They made a lonely sound. He reached to the back. There was a carton there, a brand of fine American cigarettes. He pulled it out from behind the dishes careful not to knock them out. The carton felt too light to be lucky. He wondered why he had an urge to allow, no, to *insist*, on others reading his thoughts, knowing his mind and knowing his soul. He put his hand in without looking, instead watching the clock on the wall as it transformed into a hairless ticking navel. The carton was empty.

By the time he sat down he had decided to stand up again, and put his shoes on, then his raincoat, attaching the hood, zipping it up and patting his pocket for his keys.

Samstag left the flat and entered the stairwell. He looked up the staircase and down, leaning over the flaking banister to peer down the well. He saw what he thought was a large hand gripping the rail low on the first floor, where the landlady lived, but he was mistaken. The light entering the windows shone bright and dark, shaping out a figure toward the bottom of the stairway. With a hand on the wall he made his way down the steps, tiptoeing gently so as not to creak the floorboards any more than necessary. A door closing above him, footsteps on their way. He looked up again with a start and quickened his pace, looking up, then down, frantic, not knowing where the sounds were now coming from. Was it a hand down there? Could he hear the sound of a reporter's footsteps making their way, boot on wood, up the stair? He panicked, knowing what the man in the black uniform would do if he caught him. It would be the hood all over again. It would be the black and the sickness. It would be the end again for Samstag.

(EXT. OFFICE BLOCK - DAY)

I went into the ground floor and looked up and down the list of office holdings. It was easier without all the hair in my eyes. I had cut it off the night before with a pair of long kitchen scissors in preparation for the interview. Where is it, I searched the company name without finding. But it was there.

Interviews were a delight. I derived some pleasure from exacting a type of petty revenge on the interviewer and questioned *them* instead of the reverse. Always in the knowledge that arrogance thrilled them in a kind of masochistic way.

It began as usual. Sit down, polite, be personable. Show teeth.

Hi there.

Hello, hello. Please take a seat (pointing out one of the two there). A pause. You have a very interesting CV, Mr. Sonntag. May I call you Arthur?

Arthur's fine. I sit in the offered chair. What do I call you?

Well, call me Nick.

Ok Nick nice to meet you. Smiles.

So. (Quick look over the sheet, not really looking but thinking – bring it back to zero – time is an investment.) I think you're certainly fully qualified for the job but (flash teeth, look down) I see here you were unemployed for the last tax year.

That is correct.

Why was that?

I was working on a personal project.

What was that, if you don't mind me asking?

Well I do mind you asking (I don't say that). Well, it's quite interesting actually and I think quite revealing of my hard-working nature. My driven character.

Oh yes? Peering now with slimy verve.

Yes, it was a scientific experiment I undertook. The

building of an oscillator. To generate free electricity for the borough. I fed him the enigma.

An oscillator?

Yes, well, I won't go into detail now but it was a complicated project to say the least. And all for the betterment of the community, I assure you.

Can you really not tell me any more about it? I'm very interested in gadgets. The worm turning.

Perhaps another time, and yourself, where do you see the company going? I want to be a hand on a moving ship, you see, not anchored in the harbour.

But of course, don't we all.

I used to think so.

So then he went on, the telautomaton whirring low frequencies from his speaker box.

We shook hands firmly, he over-compensating with an eager grip.

I got the job and started the following Monday.

CHAPTER FIVE

Strange brews I stirred with truth, anger and even a certain amount of harmony. Harmony driven hard to the wind and caught in the updraft with no tragedy thereafter. Anger exists in the state of mind obsessed with the future. Bitterness linked with the past. Contentment and joy found in the Now.

They say a writer can't write after drinking and/ or under the influence. But granted, they do say a lot of things. All of it some sick revelry in the concerns of others. And some of it just mystifying invention. They want a story they can tell easily and reduce it all to reason and rationale. Those words on the page represent the abyss but come from the cutlery of pens in the writer's collection, through the soft poking eyes under a furrowed brow, a kneaded chin. The pen held with a sublime grace but driven in deep only to scratch, not cut, nor slice. The typewriter's keys tapped at drifting pace, crescendos with a ring. The sage breathes no more, staring out through the cracked pane.

Disturbing voice, distracting. The ringing in the ears. A voice from the horizon. It reminds me of what I think I am looking at. A sombre tourism rested and perched on stone slabs, of outsiders photographing locals. Mocking the insider. Spaces assigned for the old men to walk and sit, chat about the minor things but really mean it. A place for security to watch. A place to sweat. To sweat, the shoe shiner knows. He gets the most sleep out of all of us.

We're wobbling out of life, flailing at all threads and on-comers, laying out fierce attacks on character, without showing the mask behind the face. The room is white spots and stricken black lines, like the sky in the mind of Munch. A forbidding last wait. Unintelligible power lines, streaming away. Always away, it seems. From her. Like the buses filled with eyes. Chugging on out. Kneeling on the back seats trying to let it go slow, easy. But only for prolonged pain. A pain that some prolong for years, for lives. The ears of wheat slipping and evading the grip. Just bare straws swaying in solemn breeze, reminding me of constant flux. I can't hold onto it too long, it kills. Though if I did I could be beating victorious hearts, as a horned Viking, determined and stubborn even if it is unmistakable burglary. It leaves a burnt sensation in the top of my mouth. Blistered. I don't know if I should end it now or later.

Waiting in the toilet cubicle. I sat on the seat motionless. The lid down, my eyes wide, shocked. I played with the toilet roll hanging out of the dispenser, pulling a piece at a time and folding each piece over the next, still looking dead ahead. All to give my neighbour the impression I was finishing up. Someone sat in the next cubicle, the toes of their black shoes visible under the raised partition. Their breathing steadied, they seemed to be listening. Monitoring my activity, listening closely to what I was up to. The tips of those black leathers did not move or shuffle. Not once. Something was up. No one can excrete with such inertia.

No sound. Can't allow it to be audible. I wet my finger on my lips, dipped my finger into the vial and rubbed it along my tongue through the bitter and the sweet. I ripped off another piece of roll and hit the dispenser with my elbow for effect. The belt in the next toilet jangled upon the tiles as the man stood up. Relief. I took out my wallet and pulled out a card, then another to crumble it up. I poured a little from the vial and watched it, careful not to fuck it all onto the floor, to which I would then have to lower and chunk it up with the dirt and the bleach residue. A nostril on the tiles. But I was careful. Slow. I tapped it, so as not to make a noise recognisable to the man now flushing his intestine down around the bend. The splashes gave perfect cover to knock out a skid on the one card, then placing the other on my knee to slowly roll the note. Solemn flushing. I preferred the note to the straw, there's no excuse for a straw, and you lose less that way. But you always lose a little.

Up it goes.

Tingle.

Burn.

Blinking watery eyes. Tingling. Excitement. Boredom.

Moving back through the white corridors my strength and resolve feeling as if it had been chipped away, gradually, my mind chiselled into a spike.

Half an hour later I'm back there. Someone's pissing onto the urinal cakes. Blue soaking up yellow. I hear them shaking out and tightening the trousers and the belt and, finally, neglecting to wash the hands.

I'm up again.

Down.

Bloodshot eye.

Sitting behind a desk, turning the screen to the wall no one sees. No work, just pretend. Entering the zone. Type type type. Silence. Noise.

Out of the sky falls everything. The hut, at a speed that ordinarily might crash it on impact, zips down and instead rests. The hammock, into the hut. The wooden slats that lead from one shelter to the next. The path leads to a mosquito net, a bed. Jungle, dense. Always dark, I look up to the night for hope of the moon. It is there but blurred. The brew has forced me to the ground. My limbs ache and the sickness runs through me as I sink lower. A train. I cannot stand up. Giving up the struggle I let it take me down stream.

Here there is no chance for black in the closed eye-socket vision. As if staring into a well of negative fire, a distance so near it appears instantly in my head, possibly emanating from there. I reach my hand trying to touch the kaleidoscope of colour. My hand is not moving. In my vision there is a cage, a round one that thinks it is not a cage at all. More of a podium. A stage for a performance. There is a silhouetted figure, dark, with long hair, and dancing. The colours surround the bubble. The fire, the green, the blinks of yellow and the stream of orange. They intertwine, serpentine hues, around the dancing shadow. I decide not to attach any meaning to the vision.

Where I stand now, is certainly a tomb. I think the world is a tomb, so I do not know whether it is the world, or a bona fide tomb, dark and bricked. I am kidnapped from the upper world to the under. An extraordinary rendition. I see a lake. Certainly black. But my vision lets it be anything but. It has no flow, of north to south, nor east to west. It is still. I dip my hand in and it holds on. It is thick. Oily. There, a bubble. It disappears. The woman strides by, looks at me. She is no longer held in the cage. The morbid lake keeps me quiet.

A dull gray nocturnal wind sweeps through the cracks of colour.

In the corner, hours later. There is a spider. It is giant

*but not bigger than I. It has long hairy legs bent upward
and down, holding it firmly in its place. As I make my approach it recedes to nothing.*

*There is a child, it raises its hand. Behind it I see a
poor, muddied face laughing. It wears a desperate com-
plexion. Shows teeth. I say:* you are not an 'it'. *It says:* yes,
I am.

Later, I find myself in the room. I am alone. I am not
laughing. My face is sullen. Ashed. I squeeze my knees
together. I rack it up again and there's a knock at the door.

*A long time and short numbers on the list, my name is
at the bottom. The recurring nightmares. I begin to shake.
Shaken into a vision. A vision of white and of black. A
clear cut horizon. Above it, only white, below it, the black.
Along the crisp line flies some winged beast. I cannot
make it out. I may be on its back. I cannot tell. It burns
along at a distance too far for my mind to see. It does not
flap, but sails something horrible, its wings dirty, the flesh
peppered with holes. It makes a strange moribund sound.
A yelp known as death. Clipping along at a steady pace,
for a while perfectly balanced between the white and the
black.*

Then its head starts to dip and its body follows.

*It sails smoothly beneath the clear-cut horizon, taking
the white with it.*

*It begins to fall, under the horizon, flying at its steady
pace, down toward the darkness.*

I can only watch and understand what it is trying to tell me.

I sit up with a snap, bursting sweat from my limbs. In a panic. I am wheeled out onto the tin pan alleys around some sort of correctional facility. Each short-legged one running foot over toe, tail over neck, like an ache of wanting more of something fake, something real and wrenching the electric engines. Eye with burnt iris and drowning whites. And singing in webs of waste silently crumbled by fingertips of thunder.

We couldn't end any type of guilt, I didn't say sorry for any type of heathen prophecy, or even the opposite. We had nothing and could only leave pen drips of pencil scratchings on empty stomachs. I was never angry any other time than when hungry. And the only time I was ever hungry was when I needed to be hungry. And she told me once, as she lay, feet crossed on sharp grass on a small knoll that led down to the water's edge, talking like a poet, though that word cringed every bone and all the tissue of me, all the atoms ... said she, she can't perform when she's eaten. She works a whole lot better on an empty tank, her belly growls along with the words, hungry to end it and feed. I looked at her knowingly, knowing I would remember her words, her voice. Those lips.

I looked back out onto the lake and wanted her to shut up.

I wasn't going back to the crying room. I wanted calm. No noise. Just water and the quack of ducks would be fine.

Later, the job is gone. I don't mind so much. I couldn't have both: the chance to do something or the balls to not want to.

CHAPTER SIX

(EXT. BEDROOM - DAY)

So there I am.

That's you and this is me. Starting fresh.

As relevant a time as any.

I sit here like a painful memory.

(INT.)

Excuse me. Father figure, how long is a day? Twenty-four hours, how come? *What is 'quest'?* What do you mean? *... and how long is a lifetime? How long is ever? I want to understand you, Father figure. And how long is the night? I don't know if you know.* Shut up.

(EXT. BEDROOM - NIGHT)

In a secluded park. Emptied of everything. No trees, no rails, no benches, I stand and watch the hollow sun resting slowly down into night. I see crumbs on the paths that snake and meet in between and flow out again, rivers of cement. Dried. Cracked. Broken. The crumbs are swept up into a breeze and fly upward into the sky. They are gone. There is no wildlife. There are no bent fingers leaning with leaves. I look into my Self and it is not there.

The Old Man watches. Some deafening, morbid thing thunders overhead.

(INT.)

In a distant land, I build my self a fortress.
I am feeble, yet ferocious in power.
I am lost, yet stretch to the skies.
I rise when darkness dies.

(EXT. CITY STREET - NIGHT)

Time was closing in on me, thirty-two and nothing of any worth in print, never will be. No job, no car, no woman. Back to normal. Back to zero. Yet failure was a haunting. The torment always keeping on at me: All the greats, painted on marble walls, started out young, a burning ambition in them to write. To create. Some had even finished by now. And don't all those trivial facts make for a great little biography in some encyclopaedia? (Published at a young age, then re-writing the holy scriptures by age thirty.) Like all those others, I wanted to start when I was fresh, to get in and say what had to be said. The truth, if there was such a thing, something new, an expression of my freedom. Maybe all those lofty ideals but probably just something a lot dirtier and simpler. Because as soon as it started to spew out of me and onto a page, the words simply clotted and died. Line after line of agreeable ideas. Nothing fresh. There were no living words on the sheets I filled. It all stank of rot. Meaning-less notepads that meant nothing to anyone, not even the countless other failures. Rot and decay. No writing of mine spoke like self-belief or confidence that shone on everybody else's words. It was all a dead language I had learnt and now could not deliver. Only in my head could I send out any messages; only in my imagination could I create something. Something could not be created from nothing, it was all just synthesis of already existent ele-ments. I took inspiration, drawn from my perceptions, and plagiarised from my heroes.

The hard work of actually writing it down seemed too much. I had been weaned on ideas of instant grati-fication and I wasn't letting them go too easily. I had fed my self with haughty ideas of proper spelling, punctua-tion, grammar. Nothing spelt out stupidity to me as eas-ily and quickly as a poorly lettered word. This proved to me beyond all else that my notions were immaculate, perfect, finished and dead. I told my self that if I ever started working hard then I must've been working for someone else. Never wanting that, I sat and did noth-ing, composing symphonies of dreams in my head, epic delusions that I would never admit to in front of anyone I cared for. And even the ones I didn't. They were all the same. It's hard to grow out of what you have learnt, it was so deeply ingrained that losing it would be like los-ing your self, whatever that may feel like. The idea was discomforting, I was surrounded by luxuries that kept me where I was and kept me 'who' I was. I didn't need anything to complicate the facts. Convenient and list-less. So I held on, as long as it would let me, as long as it could hold out.

(INT.)

Early mornings, the rarity that they are, bring re-newed verve. Awakening like the mechanical armies that litter pavements and fill buildings, we consume refresh-ing juices from inexhaustible maids, as cleaners and re-ceptionists take their posts. The uniforms rising at these hours move through the city like worn out nibs across a page. Some stand like horrified scarecrows waiting, to cross the road or enter some building, structures feeding on the marrow of depravity and exploitation. And then there are also those waiting at the wheel, for the changing lights to move on home and to bed, away from the sordid night they leave behind. Vacant memories of some sweet thing in their arms, momentarily. Leaning on that gear stick, each movement a test of stamina and the aching eye sockets.

They are all part of the rich machinery. The soiled tap-estry woven between memories and history. Coming out at them like quivering dung beetles, hiding in the darkest corners, alone but together. We wait to sleep again, and know it will not be long enough until we slip into eter-

nity's slumber, where we all have our number, resting on final mattresses – used and unused holes in mounds of earth that call our names and name our places, and the years, in petty expectancy of the next. But not everyone is celebrated in life or death. The final relax of all those temporarily strained sinews and tense tendons. We don't appreciate the momentary nature of these pains for we expect more for less, or some notion of what we are owed, and they're ideas we deserve to keep if we refuse to look any further. The souls of this city are left wanting nothing too much. Only survival.

The world is a blueprint, a draft, squared out like spaces on some giant allotment. Vast arid soil amongst dust and consistent fetters juxtaposed with palaces of dirt and carefully tended blades. We look on all sides, see these materials and the tools that maintain them.

Some want a piece of it all. Others expect nothing. Then there is all that rests between, and above. Waiting for obliteration or relief. And it will come like the Rapture.

Unfulfilling and maladroit.

That was always me, sitting there, papers on my lap, scratching out all the useless description or at least trying to catch the bits that make the heart ache with shame when you read them back. Sheer private embarrassment.

You've got to have belief though, a little bit of self-reliance, because if you haven't got that then I guess you're under control. And any loose university education might tell you that Old K-hole had a point, and *no way was I working for the machine*. What a weak exclamation.

I was on the shadowgraphing mission. In those lecture theatres, where we all became polarised, you either went one way or the other, you either fought or you subsided. You treated the classics with respect, you didn't think, you learnt. Plato was a noble statesman, not a fascist, of course. All the thinkers that are quoted and commemorated in schoolbooks and on television, they are only a cult to the regimented minds. Outside of that you had subversives, and they weren't worth your attention. You got in with the money club or you stood at the fringe not wanting any part, but secretly wanting it, at least until later when you got old enough and fed yourself enough excuses to believe you were just idealistic then, you had no responsibilities like you do now. And if you get to be like that for too long then you've surely forgotten what you wanted to do in the first place, and you're just being lead along on a piece of string.

I sat and breathed in a cigarette, the superfluous man holding the little stick of his grand revolt. To write something lasting would be satisfaction. Utter validation. I had the will to refuse mediocrity and comfort. Cast it all aside for something stirring.

But I was back in the strangled-up bedsit. A small place where one is forced to watch his Self meander, nothing else to see but his own separated body parts. Celibacy worked for Tesla, and Huxley too. They required only platonic relationships for their cerebrotonic personalities, based in a kind of spiritual but still worldly love, while they lived and worked unchained in the cave. And they were the geniuses, what might be defining of the term true visionaries. Huxley used. Tesla did not. Days haunted by the death of his older brother at a young age, he found his compulsions addiction enough. He barely ate, slept little. But he harnessed electricity and used that as a stimulant. The shock anti-therapy of cocaine. The drug akin to beeps of electricity angled straight into the brain.

And though we deluded ourselves, all day and every day, a gift such as that could never be squandered, there was no such thing as squandering the gift of genius, because it came out no matter what it faced. It would always be there. There were no gifted ones left behind, if it existed then it came forward and claimed itself, either for ego or better. The same could never be said of the mediocre and starved priests and preachers, who were looked to as if they offered the answer. The great all-encompassing answer that was the sky. They were of a different and weaker mind, a malleable flesh, terrible and pathetic, an altogether more manipulable force and prone to the ease of simple answers.

Simple, but not necessarily easy. And that was probably their most fatal flaw.

It was just when I was about to give up that I began talking again. Any stranger would do. I asked them questions, about their lives, their secrets, though they weren't always keen to oblige. Some kind of invader questioning their existence, not always welcome I suppose.

I hadn't been sleeping much when I first met Joe the Knife. At the time I mostly found shelter in inner city parks, climbing the gates by night and sleeping under the bushes. I held my blade with a fierce grip whenever I lay down. Every rustle or brush of a leaf startled me; horrible faces came out of the darkness through my imagination. The night, haunting my evenings. Perhaps Joe was just one of them. An apparition that emerges slowly when the eyeballs start to dry up and the brain begins to swell.

But Knife, he was a real piece of nowhere. So much so that even feeling sorry for him made you feel like a fool, or a pervert. When I first talked to him I couldn't believe the things he was telling me. He had been put away for sexual assault seven years previous. And the time away hadn't rehabilitated him. That much was certain. The filth that poured from his mouth made me blush.

He had a penchant for old women. That was his

thing. And that was what they had done him for in the end, or the beginning, whatever he called it now. He'd lost his job, his family, his life as he knew it when they collared him. They took it all away and tried to cut him down to fit. But there was nothing doing.

As he spoke to me with the delirious and dazzling eyes telling of horrors that to me were fortunately unseen, I got the feeling something horrific had happened to little Joe when he was a boy. I never asked. And I never held the notion too long. But there was something to like about him despite the grimy feeling you felt when you sat near him for too long. He could recite long verses of poetry from nowhere, profound words, not his own verse, but who owns words anyway. I felt a certain respect for someone who had that gift to wear the mask and speak through someone else when chance allowed. His favourite was *The Future.* By Leonard Cohen. There was something about the way his mouth curled when he said *crack* and *anal sex* and *sticking it up the hole in your culture* that made you really understand that song. And really understand that Joe really understood that song.

He used to recite a little before we became more than friendly acquaintances. Then he cut that out and started telling me about himself. There was no messing. He had tried to rape an old mare in the changing rooms of some large clothing store and by the sounds of his tale, which was empty of any regret, he had gotten pretty far. When he told it he just emptied the words out like pouring pebbles from a bucket. He could read the disgust on my face when he began his story, but there was something in his head that just didn't register disgust. His phantasies were his own and in his perfect world his behaviour would be forgettable.

They want it too you know, he told me. *It don't make no difference who or what or when.*

His way of talking whilst flicking through his merchandise gave him the casual air of some kind of survivor in a world conceived without his input. The eyes rolling back in his head, he just plodded along, trying to keep at it, selling his wares (pirated DVDs) to anyone that had comparable flavours of fetish to his.

I often gave him money, not for the pornography but because I liked to give him the impression that I was quite a well-to-do and educated young man, a prolific novelist yes, had written on all subjects really, gathering material for my next piece, a great romance. Something for the ages. Yes.

He ate it up.

I'm gonna write a book, too. He said, looking around him. Then he looked into me. With eyes that begged for purpose.

What half-complete invention am I? He said. These streets will be on the pages. I used to be rich you know. I used to have it all. All of it. Right here. His eyes searched, wistful and nostalgic, while his finger pointed to the palm of his glove. But it don't bother me none that it's all gone. Did I really lose anything? Or did I gain everything?

Depends what you want out of it, doesn't it?

That was my little trick, to ask a question without any definitive reply. But he always came back with one:

We all want the same stuff I think. Not the waxed cars or the spider-legged women, that all comes later.

He had been sent off again. You give a vagrant the time of day and they repay you with the whole of theirs. Constantly blurting.

It's the sense of winning the race. At least being a part of it and running your lane, stickin' to it – not botherin' none about the others. He looked me through the eye and raised his Tenant's Super.

But we can't ignore the others can we? He sipped. I looked at the soiled pavement beneath my feet as my hands searched my coat for a cigarette.

They learn Rimbaud too early in France, he remembered someone tell him. He repeated the thought: too early teaches them to hate it. School's no time for real, genuine thought, he repeated in his head. Only after school do they realise an appreciation. All the books. The books. Show of teeth.

The cigarettes. They came in handy during the awkward moments, like putting up a barrier of smoke between you and the world, a temporary cage of isolation, perceptibly secure. I did one. Enjoyed it for a bit. Stubbed it out.

Knife recited more poetry, gushing as he cupped my shoulders with his chubby paws. I sat rigid, staring off and out of my head. My mind. These places that wouldn't dissolve without effort.

Sometimes I listened, and sometimes I dreamt.

CHAPTER SEVEN

When Samstag returned, his coat and his shoes were drenching wet. The soles schlupped as he stepped onto the welcome mat, soaked with the drip of sky. He looked from the hallway through the living room and out the window. In the second floor flat across, the blinds were drawn right up, but the light of day reflected any view back out onto the street, revealing nothing. He checked the other windows, all the same and saw that the curtains were still drawn.

Removing his coat and his shoes, he took out a fresh cigarette and lit it. Smoke billowed from his downturned mouth and rose up the coat and the wall. He laid down the sealed cartons.

He walked over to the window and sat on the chair positioned there, which rarely moved. From his lookout point he saw more window and more wall.

The chair in which he sat, positioned by the window, now on the third floor.

He pushed open the glass and tapped the ash, wondering how this had occurred without his noticing. He looked down to the street below and leaned all the way over the ledge, half his body hanging outside the building. He was closer to the ground now. There was no way the fall could kill him from here. He tapped the ash and pulled on it again. The sweet release. He leaned down again thinking the fall probably wouldn't even paralyse him. It wasn't high enough. He would probably leave a red splat on the pavement, crooked legs splintering out from under his abdomen, but he would survive it, even crawl away. The window below seemed close. The street closer. If there were a fire he would be able to jump down there by gripping this ledge and swinging to the next. He shrugged his shoulders as if to an audience. No one could see him. Only tourists look up. And they were a rarity. That was all he could think, looking through the smoke. The smoke. He would survive a fire. If he fell, yes, he would probably survive. But it would look like an accident. No one would seriously consider suicide from the third floor.

He manoeuvred his body back into the room and finished the cigarette, being careful not to watch across now that he was visible and somehow closer. He pretended to look more interested in the street below, or just indifferent to any of it. A glance at the sky. It ignored him. *Oh, me? Just having a cigarette*, he thought. A wasp flew from behind and knocked against the window seeing its escape, but couldn't reach it. Samstag innocently closed one door of the window, leaving the other open to breathe in hot air.

He raised a month old newspaper from the table and read over its yellowy pages. The wasp buzzed and jutted up along the window frame. He looked at it then looked back to his paper. He saw his name on the front page: 'By Niall Samstag.' He read over the words, their words, but felt shame instead of pride at the copy he had filed. He flicked to the inside page where he read his name again, the pain of it beating into his belly and the not knowing why made it more excruciating. He lit another cigarette as if the plain activity of it might distract. He pulled deep on the filter and held the smoke in his chest until only a whisper of it could breathe out. For twelve years the pride had built up in him, the joy of success, the satisfaction of arrival, mounted with a gradual realisation that stalked him as he stared emptily.

His mediocrity soaked his hands, his sleeves, all of it emanating from the browning paper. Had he become that last man? He thought maybe that it was a gradual transition, and that it wasn't too late to turn it around.

He reflected on the way he had deluded himself into believing his role. The role he undertook was one of self-importance. Serious, earnest-looking, in all those mandatory professional profiles. Another layer of something to protect you from the truth. And a belief that what he was doing could not be overcome. There was nothing outside of it and nothing greater. Conquering even time.

The wasp walked on the windowsill, exhausted, struggling up to the window but not buzzing, not flying. How could it have taken so long to realise what had become of him? The wasp tracked up the windowpane then slipped and fell, done for. One half of the window was still open. Yet he stuck to the one pane, staying inside the frame. He seemed to know he would not escape, too myopic to see the open frame right there next to him.

Speaking with colleagues was a haughty illusion. Everything had already been said, they understood things only the one way. These conversations: He could somehow seep out of his eyes and watch his mouth moving, then the opposing lips, with only silence spoken.

Sitting up, he waited, three nights in a row. The hours, and then the days, rolling into the next, when time ceased to tick but instead slid out from under him without alarm. The wasp rested.

The flashes reflected off the glass of his eyes. Staring at television, the rays beaming through the sockets of his skull. He sat there, a hand laid neatly and gently on each of his rotting knees, like the altar boy looking down at the stupefied congregation, all sitting softly with their hands in their swelling laps or with their hands on their swelling Books. As the polemics came rushing toward them.

Televisual images of stoning, beating, whipping, stabbing, spearing. Afternoon programming. The rapine and grim murder, glanced off his brain into the ether. From where it came, he never pondered. His ragged yellow curtain, giving way to new morning rays, looked ready to fall earthwards, unveiling an entire world outside his darkened chambers.

But the world was closed and closer to him now, he was on the other side of the golden archway, so seldom seen but so commonly felt. He wondered if he had ever been on the right side. He had waited, like every man, for some mark of change – a new way. A beam to lift him.

(INT.)

I remember pockets and windows emptied of light, mullions on windows standing solemn. A brief freelance opportunity had arisen and I had seized it sideways. At least I was on my way. The employer, the editor: heartless and unbound by moral shoestrings and not reliant on any slow ethics. Or at least some of them. It was never clear to me what rules he professed to live by. We're professionals, he would say. You're a professional, I'm a professional. Or glorified salesmen. A butler in the house of cards, piling on the trimmings for the foie gras buffet.

He showed me an insincere delight in offering out the assignment, like it was some kind of triumph and, despite his sporadically rolled-back eyeballs, I accepted.

Right, there's been some kind of abduction. The lat-

est in a long line. We're running some features on them
now there's been a number of them, enough to justify
it. We've got a string of local celebrities coming out to
say kidnapping's wrong and all that. You know the kind
of stuff. If you need help take a look at the stabbings bit
we ran last year. Same old thing, just throw in some of
the real stuff. You know, locals and that talking about it.
Emotions. Bothering their nappies about it all.

Sure.

Good then. It happened over by the high-rises just
out in Suburbiton. Young lady, 32. No children according to our sources. And I want copy by yesterday.

He gave a stomach laugh. A bellyful of bile jiggling
at me.

Yes, sir. My cheeks taut in a smile. A pair of teeth.

Try and blow it up a bit, you know what I mean. Get
the spicy bits down and then make them fucking spicier.
You know what I mean. Wink. Ask the right questions.
We want the scum locked up in cages over this one. And
if not, people baying for it at least. We can run with this
for months.

I nodded in the drift.

The sublime knowledge inherent in this kind of work
is, as you might expect, completely down to one single
accord. One notion that aligns itself through every moment of your tenure. The accord that never shifts despite
constant flux, like the psychic awareness and percep-

tion of some objective realisation in a fifth dimension. Besides the bullshit, it's like this: You don't have to do anything. You can quit at any time. Give it up. End it.

The same with anything.

And that is what I believed, the idea I lived by. So instead of doing 'something', it would be 'nothing'. Cut and paste and twist. Other sources. Pick out the flesh between the teeth. And even if it was 'something', it was really nothing.

I just didn't take my self as seriously as them.

They believed in convergence, convergence like nothing else. All into the same hyperbolic cliché without any sense of meditation or conference.

Every article, every story, was like the last and the next, same overblown morals shot in your face with the machine-gun-gutter journalism. That was fine. No more unpaid labour. No more free *content*.

This time, the cheque was in the post.

CHAPTER EIGHT

(EXT. STREET - DAY)

I went down to the scene and stared into the contorted face of the building. It reminded me of her. It was gray, looked dead.

I shook it off, almost wondering where she might be now. All had been taken care of. Nothing to worry about. Swallow the guilt.

I went around to the side of the block, the birds watching there and floating about, landing then taking off, teasing the ground. Two assaulted each other atop a low wall that ran beside the entrance, on the perimeter of the looming townhouse. The playful creatures pecked at each other's bills, flapping their wings, struggling to hold ground on the wall as the dominant male, a dirty white with brown-tipped feathers, kept the other at a wing's length by sharp digs to the neck, their angled beaks flashing. Blurs of gray, white-brown beaks, squawks and red eyes. A pleasant hate triangle conjured between them.

The female watched the two. Her head faced forward, away, but her watchful eyes capturing it, perched silent on the far end of the wall. The gray took off as I entered the building, moving up the four steps. Gray knew it wasn't worth the bother.

My neck pinched tight as it turned to take in a final look of the exterior.

The flight of the female blew past the wide framed door, in the same direction, as my eyes returned to look at the floor. The hallway had been freshly mopped, the smell of chemical heat rising up my nostrils. I reached in my pocket for a kerchief to cover my nose.

Short breaths. Don't take it in. Deadly odour.

(INT.)

I looked up the stairwell and saw a face peering down. Then it swept away, the lengthy brown coat disappearing obediently behind. The well was silent now. The face was young, frightened, ghostly. It had darted out knowingly, spying me as I stood there below. I could hear its timid breath unsuccessfully held back, in between chirping birds and gusts that cars threw out behind them.

Another door shut, a dull bang reaching the summit of the well and back down. Faint but audible. Footsteps worked their way round the top of my head, far above but getting closer. Creaks of wood gave way to tread. I heard the startled young man in the long coat skip a few steps then enter a doorway, swift and quiet. But not silent. The door clicked shut. The boot-steps beat their sound down the staircase, tip-toeing on my skull. A man in a black jacket, dark trousers and high-laced boots met me at the bottom and gave me an upward nod, his gloves still gripping the rail leading down.

An officer, eh? He said.

Is it that obvious?

Yeah. Your shirt. And one o' them jackets. He pointed at my long coat.

Well what's a reporter doin' in here? I asked, feigning a common tongue.

Just askin' questions, you know the drill. You'll probably read that report later, no doubt. Had anuver complaint from some old bag up top. Fuck knows 'ow she gets up there everyday. Don't look like she leaves that hole much to be fair.

What's she moanin' about?

Says she saw sumfing again. Where that abduction happened. Buildin' across innit. You know the one? She's been watchin' it ever since. Scared shitless 'bout the whole fing.

What d'you make of it?

Who knows. Don't ask questions, me. Just get in, get out, get home, get quietly plastered. Ha.

Ha ha, yeah. I laughed with him some more. I was just goin' up there myself. Did she witness the actual kidnapping?

Says she did, who knows. Old hags lark 'er say a lot o'

fings. You 'avin a look fer yerself, are ya?

Not for myself, for the paper.

Wot one?

The O Press.

Not bad, not bad. Pays the bills innit. Only read the reds me. Fuckin' joke wot's happened round 'ere it is. Fuckin' joke.

It is innit? Keeping up the charade. Continuing the bumble of lad-uage. He didn't seem to be falling for it.

Anyway, I'm headin' off. Good luck wiv 'er.

Cheers, I said.

Later geez. He said as he passed. Oh, one more fing. He said, turning back. Wootn't drink any of 'er tea. Cat piss, the lot of it.

Thanks for the warning, I said to the disappearing figure. Goon, I thought. Fucking goon. I walked up the stairs.

No sign of that lad from before. Guess he decided to stay home for the day. Can eat his legs for supper. His foot for breakfast. I made my way past and climbed to the top floor. Last door on the right. I knocked, the paint shedding some flakes with each jolt.

Eventually: Yes? A small voice from behind the door.

Hello, Miss Potter. I'm Arthur Sonntag from the local paper, I spoke with you on the phone?

What was your name again?

Sonntag. Arthur Sonntag.

When did I speak to you?

This morning, about 10 o'clock.

And you say your name's? Arthur, is it? That was my husband's name.

Would you mind letting me in, Mrs Potter?

Oh yes, yes. The frail words got nearer the door as her thin fleshless hand unlocked and unchained the latch.

I stood rigid and smiled.

Come in come in. Would you like a cup of tea?

No, thank you, just had one at the office. All day in there, cooped up. Drink nothing but tea every ten minutes.

Oh, are you sure? I just made a fresh pot. A nice man from the Metro Polis station was just in here. He didn't want none either.

Yes, thank you, Mrs Potter. Do you mind if we get right to it? I didn't wait. May I ask what your first name is?

Why do you need it?

For the article, Mrs Potter.

Oh yes, of course. It's Clarisse. C-L-A-R-I-S-S-E. Clarisse.

Okay. Thank you. I made a note in the flip pad. Shall we take a seat?

Sure, sure, help yourself. Would you like a cup of tea?

Erm, no thank you Mrs Potter, still not.

Oh are you sure? I just made a fresh pot. Nice fellow from the Metro Polis was just up here, asking me some questions. He didn't drink any either. She shook the china in an attempt to entice me, the liquid almost over-flowing. Go on, there's plenty.

OK, go on then, I'll have a cup.

Fantastic. I'll just go get you one. You can ask me any questions you like, Mr…?

Arthur.

Oh, Arthur. That's a lovely name. My husband's name was Arthur.

Oh, really? That's fascinating.

Yes, isn't it?

There's a lot of us about.

She edged her way over to the kitchen with small steps, through the hall. I heard her carefully picking out a cup, setting it down and pouring in the tea. A brown fluff of cat brushed by my leg, looking up at me with its piss-coloured eyes. I waited for her to return, her small steps reduced further by her cargo of a silver tray, a saucer beneath the cup and a small plate of half-crumbled biscuits beside.

Here you go. She spoke as she set it down.

I might as well leave, I thought to my self. Her memory's blitzed, and I can barely breathe with all the rot in here. Should have made the quotes up back at the office, she'd never know.

So what is it that you saw, Mrs Potter?

Please. Call me Clarisse.

Yes, so what is it that you saw, Clarisse?

Well, of the kidnapper?

Fine, yes, we can start with the kidnapper.

I really already told all of this to the Metro Polis. Do you need it again?

Yes, I'm dealing with a slightly different thing here.

Oh, different how?

Well, I need a few words from you, your side of the story.

Ohhhhh. But what good's it going to do anyone having a little old lady like me in your paper?

She had a point, but I gave her the spiel anyway.

You're not just a little old lady. You're someone readers can relate to. You're someone people can identify with. And we have to give the people a voice. A say. The news is very democratic that way. And don't you want to see your name in the paper anyway? Won't that give you a thrill? You can tell all your friends. Your grandkids. It'd give them a kick.

Oh, I don't know about that. Not nice to be in the paper for something like this, is it? Maybe if I won a raffle, that would be nice, but. She looked down at the tea and biscuits, then looked up again at me. Are you going to catch the kidnappers?

There was more than one kidnapper?

Yes, I saw two men. Yes, two. Two. Both in balaclavas

all wrapped up like it was cold as winter.

Can you describe them?

Well, I couldn't see much to be honest. My eyes aren't what they used to be. But they were big, well one of them was. The other was thin but still tall. They were both tall, yes. But one of them was a bit on the fat side. Oh, I shouldn't say that, should I? You won't call him fat will you?

Don't worry about hurting their feelings, Mrs Potter, they're most likely terrorists, or drug dealers, or gangsters. Something on the wrong side of people like you and I.

Oh really? Oh dear. I really don't think I should be getting involved in this. She shifted in her seat, I was losing her.

Don't worry, you'll be safe, you'll be fine. I'm sure they have what they want by now.

Oh, dear. She leaned back and then sat up again on the stale sofa, her hands in her lap, her knees together, looking worriedly out the window to the room a floor below hers. Winning a raffle would be nice, she said. Then: Who was the girl?

A young woman.

What did they want with her?

Well, we don't know yet, the reporters are looking into it.

What do you suppose it was?

Like I say, drugs, prostitution, something political maybe.

Oh, I see. She looked at the table again. Won't you drink your tea?

Sure, thank you. I lifted the mug and looked into its deepening, darkening recess. Looking at the bits floating, the different liquids swirling together. I held it, thinking she could just assume I was drinking it.

A biscuit?

Oh, no thank you, don't want to spoil my appetite.

Just one. Go on.

She wasn't letting up. Okay then, I said, and picked up the least grotesque-looking biscuit, a pink wafer. I held it for a moment, then dropped it by my shoes.

Mmm. Yum, thank you.

You're welcome. Help yourself. She said it proudly.

What time did all this happen, Mrs Potter?

Oh, ermmm... She was improvising. Some time around mid-afternoon.

What time would you say exactly?

Oh, I don't know.

Guess.

Well, I was just eating my lunch and I stood up to get something or other and then that's when I saw it all happening. So it must have been about three o' clock, something like that.

Right. I wrote down three pm followed by a question

mark.

And could you describe exactly what you saw?

Well, when I stood up, I could see a man in a black mask walking slowly toward the window. He was looking down at something. Then he bent over and grabbed something with both his hands. I'll never forget it. He was holding the poor girl by the hair. He dragged her across the room and threw her against the wall. It was terrifying. Real shocking it was. Then I couldn't see them after that.

Were they both throwing her about?

No, the second one was just walking around, but a couple minutes later, I'm not sure, he seemed to be looking for something, he went from room to room, you know. Searching, like. Sort of hurried, sort of frantic, he was throwing his arms about this way and that. And then... He ran over to the window and looked out. But then he disappeared, ran off somewhere, couldn't see anything after that.

Very good, Mrs Potter.

Is there anything else I can help with?

Yes, the reporter downstairs told me that you saw something else recently?

Well, yes. Last night I saw another masked man looking around again. I wrote it down so's I wouldn't forget. He was slower this time, less hurried. More careful, like.

Very good.

How come he was allowed to get in there?

It was blocked off. But the guard must have been on a break or something, or maybe they just got rid of the guard.

I haven't seen any Metro Polis around here.

Well there're supposed to be. What was he doing in there anyway? Could you see what he was doing?

Not really, but he was really calm. She took a bite of cookie, most of it crumbling around her mouth and into her lap. He was even sitting down reading at one point. But he never turned on any lights though.

And you definitely saw this man yesterday?

Well. Yes. Definitely. I wrote it down. She showed me the paper, illegible scribbles.

Ok, Mrs Potter. You've been a fantastic help. I'll get this written up and be in touch.

Oh, but you haven't finished your tea.

That's okay, thank you again.

No, you must.

Really, it's okay, I must leave now.

No, you have to finish your tea. She looked me in the eye.

Mrs Potter, I do not want your tea. Good day.

I exited, allowing the door to slam behind me. I breathed deep again. The stench still followed.

When I found my self in the open and looked up, I

had this overwhelming feeling. As if I may burst into the sky.

I took my time on the way back to the office. The story rolled itself over in my mind. I had the angle. The angle was easy. Just another unwarranted, uncalled-for kidnapping. Random crime, that was an easy jig to dance. That was enough of a hook to get papers moving, the headlines wrote themselves.

Another random kidnapping. Nothing extraordinary, though I didn't want to think about it. I stood at the end of the avenue and looked back up at the two facades facing each other, the light gray of the road between them. It would cost too much time to get to the bottom of it. Put it down to random collisions. Particles raring to combust. Volatile catalyst. The street always a catalyst.

I went down the subway stairs, watching the people move in straight and even lines, up the escalator. The train was leaving. I knew my heavy lungs wouldn't allow it, and a break was good here. Shade, no sunshine. Breeze from the tunnel. I turned the cigarette packet in my pocket over and over. Frowning and thinking. About what, I'm not quite sure. At the end of the platform, tiny figures stood glued at the opposing exit. They looked like reporters. They were conferring on something while pointing up the escalator, tracking something's movements. The train arrived. I decided to keep my nose out of their dealings. I stepped onto the first carriage and took a stained seat. As the train departed the men began walking up the edge of the platform, exaggerated stride and shoulders bent forward. I got a beam of lengthy faces, and I was gone, on the stream of light and metal moving deeper through the tunnel.

They'd been in the flat for two days now, watching the news reports on my old worn-out picture box. Silent. Most of the time silent. I didn't know how to behave as they sat there, relaxed on the sofa, sipping at dirty cups, eyes glued to it. Analysing it. Picking it apart.

Predictable. The Old Man said.

Yep, fucking typical. She said.

I watched the box, trying to comprehend what they meant. In all the time they had spent there I hadn't actually looked at the tube to realise what they were watching. I observed them in my periphery instead, preparing my self for a vicious move. I held a long and furious look. The longer they stayed the more hysterical the internal paranoia became. Every now and then she would give me a look that said *relax*, that said: *it's okay*. She was very communicative with just that pair of blue eyes. I didn't care what they wanted to do to me, if anything.

I suspected little. But as long as she looked at me with those blue eyes, it didn't matter. Fingertips needing to grip that flesh.

They've cut all footage of the cash drop. It's been sanitised. But sanitised to make it more explosive. Not one shot of the money drop. They just look like they're rioting for the sake of rioting.

Then the hypothesis was correct. I win. She smiled at him then turned back to the screen.

Surely something will come out about it. Why haven't they talked to witnesses?

Because they're all locked up or hospitalised.

A pause.

Who could believe they'd do this?

I watched the screen. He was right. The protesters were there, on the screen, at the march, hitting out at the Metro Polis who appeared only to be defending themselves. If you watched carefully you could see paper flying. But it could have been anything. Pamphlets, flyers, uncivilised propaganda. Anything at all.

Jesus. I said.

We watched in silence.

The television spoke: Several wounded Polis are still being treated in hospital today, in the aftermath of an explosive encounter with militant protesters over the weekend. Metro Polis officials say up to six of their Reporters have been severely injured in the breakout of violence. There is no excuse for this behaviour, Metro Polis spokesmen said this morning in a press conference. But campaign groups also say they expected violence to erupt at the march. Eyewitnesses claim to have seen a bombardment of paper pamphlets thrown during the clashes, but these claims are as yet unconfirmed.

Listen to this. The Old Man stood up, arms flailing in the air. We have to do something about this. Now.

What do you mean? I asked, looking to her, needing some reassurance. Those eyes.

Hit back. Hit back with our own footage.

You have footage? I asked.

They looked at me without readable expressions for a moment.

Who do we go to? We can't bring it to the Metro Polis, and I won't hand it over to the press.

Why not? I said. They'll show it. If it's genuine, solid footage, they'll show it.

They'd put us away for it.

I piped up: I can hand it in for you. I can do it anonymously. I have contacts with the O Press.

You are joking aren't you? The Old Man took his seat again. They'll butcher it and reshape it, without doubt. And even if they didn't there's too much heat on the other side for anything to happen about it. It'll just be forgotten. The Polis will get away with brutality and the protesters will get even worse treatment. Surveillance, questioning. Sentencing.

You don't know that.

Yes, I do. The Old Man looked to the girl. We have to set something else up. She looked at him, then looked back to the screen. Her eyes had unfocussed, had become watery. She stared toward the television, as if apologetic for something. The Old Man looked into me. But she kept those blue eyes hidden.

CHAPTER NINE

(EXT. OFFICE - DAY)

The editor spoke: We're continuing the Stabbings thing from last year, you know, a little catch up, find out where the victims' families are now, what the convicted are doing. It's been a year. They're all out by now. But keep it to the format, don't go investigating unnecessary areas, but maybe have a look at gangs. But definitely don't go hunting into government policy on prison terms. Old hat. Hang heavy on the father figures, and all that. Put it all down to something, yeah? Just keep it to what we know though. No think pieces, just the well-rounded facts.

And I could only whisper from my hidden stupor, vaguely inebriated on a high-chair: yessirwillbeonthatrightlyso. Each word tumbling heavily into the next and back into the one before. I was a mess. But I didn't ever want to get straight. I wanted to forget. Delude memory from all that had happened. Forget all about her and all of the cliché.

I blinked and held a look steady. There it was. The chasm between us, the editor streaming off into distance. As with all managers and employers, authoritarian and bureaucrat in the history of commerce and religion, all governments in between... it is a malevolent, naïve and fatalistic error to show this suited fop *any* of your traits, your personality. The ideas that make up the space you fill. Never treat them like a friend. Safe distances for those people. Yes, definitely safe distances. And by safe I mean it has to be on the far side of the room and keep yourself moving, across that giant confessional box.

And never let them know what happened last night. They are managers and foremen for a reason. Just the same way anyone in any position of power has taken that vocation, to heart and to hold it. Even the bus drivers and ticket inspectors, the lawmen and all the other controlling banes that exist under the cloud of this farcical carnival. They have their reasons. But I don't knock it, I just watch it. We all have to eat, to keep the slope sliding, to keep the petty victories coming. It's the same wherever you look.

I walked in, the day heavy, knowing the reports would start flying their way through the ether, and I would again become a victim of will. The first one was a Saturday. Lucky that. Lucky because of the sanctimony of Friday, that I walked in not aware of my self, not knowing that the stink on me rotted down to my shoes. Ready to walk through a wall.

Saturday to me had been taken over for the masses by the two poisoned institutions, maybe three, that hung over the first day of the weekend like an organised stench. The football and the club; both rumbling arenas of savagery and laudable occasion for celebration. The soil for the heroes of circumstance. It was all confusing. The weekends vanished and no one knew where to follow them. On that day, if it's not creation then it's most likely destruction. And even then, most of their creation reverses to the slumber of dust. And then there are those that go to church and eat it.

The blank stare is a close ally in this whole charade. Blank but also belligerent. Throw in a nod and tight lips, look through it all, maybe a sharp mmhm for when they need to know, need to feel comfortable, less awkward. That is all they need, a little encouragement. Let them think it's all important, all relevant, all coming down to the big ideas. When they run around in their two-grand suits, un-crumpled like the fabric of their cerebrums, panic and disgrace held in both hands, ask them with your eyes: When did you forget?

They could be human after all and may even consider your stare, standing gently without gall. The crux is always the wash of memory, like the last bell ringing on a Saturday night wall of imposed Alzheimer's. The age of amnesia, someone once called it. And the amnesia is convenient for those who spend their days taking the heart out of it all, then the veins the arteries the bone the marrow the tissue. But I heard they always leave the skin.

Hollowed as it is, the skin will serve a purpose for the replacement. The bone is moving everywhere.

(INT.)

Glass doors. Cold, odious. I stood around and got adjusted, looking across their desks. Paper, pens and machinery. I looked back at the editor while I walked down to that desk at the O Press for the first time. It ran across the entire room, as wide as the building itself, and upon it all manner of lost ideas.

The phone started to ring and I didn't want to answer it. I'd just arrived and already I was picking up calls for the rest of the chumps? I left it ringing for the chance of someone else foolish enough. It kept ringing.

Hello?

Hi, I'm at Shortbridge tube station. There's been a jumper, said this anonymous female voice through the telephone.

A jumper?

Suicide. I thought you should know.

Thanks?

I hung up and sat there. I sat there. This was the first thing I would have to write up. How could this woman have called up, not knowing the circumstances, magicking me straight into action by setting this in front of me?

I wondered to my self how this had just happened. No answer present.

Yeah, excuse me, there's a man under a train at Short-bridge.

Write it up.

I didn't notice the warm detachment, of things seen and reported, that naturally followed. And as soon as I loaded up a fresh page to start typing on that un-glowing screen, all my thoughts went dead. Then I started typing furiously, no thoughts, just platitude. I felt like another one of them, dialling calls to transport Polis and all the rest of them, taking down meaningless details. Should this be going out to the people? The people. Who are they? Whose responsibility is it to make this known, I thought. Someone else was going to do it anyway I decided, I might as well have a say for all the heads that read it out there in any-man's town.

We laughed about it. I understood why, but it still didn't seem natural.

Then they all started jumping. There were four in the succeeding month, and they started getting even more frequent. It was entirely my fault. Maybe someone had seen that story then decided to go out and do the same. And the same with the next, and all the others, like some over-subscribed cult of fiends. At least that's what I thought then. But I had no real reason to believe that.

The editor would often ask: What are they doing?

Doing what they have to, I said, everyone's rushing to get out.

I know, right? Always came the reply.

I don't.

But I did.

The same week I was ordered out to a stabbing. Just the one that day. Still, I was soon to find out the stabbings came on just about as frequent and savage as the men and women diving under slow-moving trains.

I went down to the decorated site. The flowers sat posing upwards, dying. And the people strolling, they all looked like plain clothes Metro Polis-men. I wandered through the area, looking into the quick-sliding eyes of the people around me. There didn't seem to be much glistening there.

I took a seat with a notepad and pen to scribble some quick ideas. It happened to be a café, quiet, so I stayed and drank a coffee. Along the shop window sat a curiously plastic-bagged man. He started on about something, told me a story. It was about how the young lad that's in questioning for this latest attack, how he once threatened him.

He said: That lad, he flashed the blade. He'd asked me what the time was and I gave it to him.

I was listening intently, it's important, I kept being told. He started talking about the threats, the serene look on the boy's face dancing with the knife that night.

He said:

I knew what to tell him, but I've been thinking about that. I don't know if I said the right thing. I told him to stab me. I told him to do it slow and deep, so that I'd feel it. He didn't believe me and continued the threats. I urged him and put my hand on the knife and squeezed the edges. I told him I was a suicider too. But he wouldn't help me. I told him it's what I needed, but he refused. He put it away, into his pocket and hung his hood over his head and ran off.

This man, this ordinary looking man that I had met by chance, accident it seemed, was laying it on, but piecing together the ideas that had been trailing me. He wanted to die; he was just like them, believed in nihil. This new breed. Again.

Don't you believe me? He asked.

I had no reason not to.

He stood there, thinking of a way to enlighten the situation. Swaying slightly.

What if I told you that I was on my way to Short-bridge to jump that day?

I didn't say anything. Had no answer. The ears began to reverberate, an engine in the street silently humming out a vibration.

So, what's out there to believe in? He was asking me now.

Nothing much.

He looked at me like I already knew.

Sometimes it's not what you say, but what you don't. Of course, that's obvious. Superficial even. Every day, people living and dying by that rule. And that opens the mind to the possibility that anything is possible. Just that, if it hasn't yet been said, is it waiting to be said? A lot of people don't think that one through all the way. They only feel through their senses.

(INT.)

I imagined a larger living space, where I would never again have to look inward, never again have to recall those early days at the O Press. Only out. But I tried with my pen. I tried so hard to cross through all the effusive words, just wanting something simple for once. No fancy trickery or wordplay if I could manage it. Just a simple message, whatever it means, that goes from A to B, using up all the words that aren't mine and sending it to a place that I'll never find. Sending it along with a little bit of life, even a little chunk of my own mind if that's what it takes. Exposing some of the absurdity, of what is in me, and what is out there.

In my trance, the cigarette went down all the way, leaking out over my jaundiced fingers. Another one gone, and still sitting there concentrating on what I think counts, I lit another one, my eyes not drifting an inch, catching my nose with the lighter a little but it didn't matter, the pen has to keep moving and the eye has to keep finding.

I was beginning to hear the sounds of the devils and the clowns laughing and jesting. Dividing my fingers. Stretched. Squeezing me into a perineum between vapidity and fertility. Turned brown round this camel's leg and stinging all the eyes above and below. Their laughter eating my teeth.

Listening to the lounge and the tunes dealt like cards, burnt out on unreasonable airs, crossing legs in terrifying silence more pointed than ever. The world angled at me, more than before. And You. It's no wonder each move lit my final candles. But the first eyes to shine a light on you, putting you in manual focus, your knees lifted in elegant shadows of your head and you're humming, in silence, the all of you moving to some blurry majesty. The television lighting your blue face.

Your eyes escaped from blackness, crawled out from under the table, and chaos. Something pure that cannot be held or owned. Under no control and half-dug deep to be hidden for when things start to roll down the dusted knolls of time passing and losing all traditions of known things, learnt to be unlearnt, formed to be destroyed.

All by the same room in a space of time indescribable

as nothing and eternity.

And the heartless many, their numbers grow fully. In the heart's core. Hollowed, all but pure. No traces of the basics. Love, remorse, anger, guilt. Psychosis sets in for so many, so many that we can't peel back anything but the lid. Holding candles for acolytes and carving new shapes on the old walls. The Petri dish infected by the scum growing on the invisible flags, directed along lines for blades and bullets. That will cut air like groans boiled in her bosom. To file all lines into hate and gather the remains in the puddles of gutters to be saved in sewers, for the only thing that can last on this grotty wall is the lick of that tongue.

Because we are all children and latch onto any one thing we can get at. To take it and put their face on it, their eyes, ears, their reality, distorted as it is: Them. On and into it. And this works with all things attached to people who subscribe to these rails of thought. Mellowing and quietening down, ultimately, 'til the end of this thing. The corridors are bare. No loitering. You choose your door on this hallway and you only have one-way keys for the lock. They won't let you back. The door opens once, each time, fast and you can't miss it. But you might, for no great reason, appreciate the truth or the answers. We are all of it. Born out and headed into it. The smaller truths: intricate. And the larger truths: plain. And we all have to find it within these boundaries. Enough to line but not nourish, necessity like the farmer and his gun.

So, collect. Collect those things when you find the arms that might hold you or lift you up. Standing, dying in the clothes that cling to you. Unstitching feeling from all the spaces that can lean to the monolith at the end of that hall. That corridor of two-way mirrors without irony. Just cold stolen death. Built in your image and within the chalk outlines around desks and beds.

We all find out things. The things that simultaneously cling to us as us to them, like feet on pedals. Or smoke and heat. We will crawl to them when the rest of the world is whipping us and our masters. We can step out from within the lights of our pupils and colours of our irises. We can choose or choose not to. We can imagine or imagine not to. And try and learn about all things. All except beneath the brows of hollowed owls and the creatures that walk dressed or shoeless. Yet we will only really understand what we know and webs of things we are told, pages rolled and wrapped to be sold, to birthing and old. For what trees will behold any standing tiptoes on cold stone or edges smoothed by mild hands that are landing around arteries that keep us above the mould. Before once more sold.

Vague trails of thought lead by inward thinking snails. But there is a new kind. Together, standing alone. Shooting guns and flashing knives into the green and blue earth. And its white heart. And simply smiling at the deck of cards and the grin of the jester within.

You could say it's pretty hard to say everything at once. A poem, a short story, even a whole book. But many have done it, and some have done it well. I guess trying to force it through a voice that says it all at the same time isn't easy. You only think it is because you have 'the gift'. A pitiful talent. What a disgrace. At the very least, it's not as simple as that. You know, finding a structure, keeping it all tight and lean, making all the right choices. When I got down to doing it myself, trying to say something, anything, I failed.

I tore the sheets of gibberish and spat on my words. There was no way for me to communicate.

Huxley, born 1894, published 1920, age 26

Dostoevsky, born 1821, published 1846, age 25

Kierkegaard, born 1813, published 1841, age 28

Rimbaud, born 1854, published 1866, age 12

Camus, born 1913, published 1937, age 24

Hamsun, born 1859, published 1877, age 18

Fante, born 1909, published 1933, age 24

Celine, born 1894, published 1932, age 38

Villon, born 1431, published 1461, age 30

Hemingway, born 1899, published 1923, age 24

Nabokov, born 1899, published 1916, age 17

Anderson, born 1876, published 1916, age 40

Miller, born 1891, published 1934, age 43

Bakunin, born 1814, published 1848, age 34

Vonnegut, born 1922, published 1950, age 28

Nietzsche, born 1844, published 1858, age 14

Lautréamont, born 1846, published 1868, age 22

Conrad, born 1857, published 1895, age 38

Tzara, born 1896, published 1916, age 20

Dick, born 1928, published 1951, age 23

Musil, born 1880, published 1906, age 26

Whitman, born 1819, published 1839, age 20

Burroughs, born 1914, published 1953, age 39

Bukowski, born 1920, published 1944, age 24

Burgess, born 1917, published 1956, age 39

Thompson, born 1937, published 1966, age 29

Kafka, born 1883, published 1904, age 21

Zamyatin, born 1884, published 1917, age 33

Pound, born 1885, published 1908, age 23

(INT.)

All the young upstarts laughed. I cowered between the shivering walls. 26.97. That makes me 5.1 past expiration.

I flicked the book open to a random page.

I obsessed about the writers; it was their lives, seldom their work, that had me so hypnotised.

Their lives, not their words, that absorbed my mind.

And I wondered why they all went blind.

It was like trying to fill a wishing-well from a dirt ditch, without a bucket. Like watching a long, tall wall in the rain, gently splashed by the sideways drops sent in by the blowing wind. Gradually the whole thing would darken and the flat orange would turn to a dark, glistening brown. I looked at my empty hands. Yet it kept on dripping in, as it has and always will. Bernays'll tell you, the well will one day overflow. The wall will get its full soaking. And you never really have much to begin with. A wall, a bucket. You begin, bucket of the mind, pouring more in, always tipping every bucketful you get, always worrying how long it takes. Just doing it because it makes you feel. Is it real? Yes or no, it doesn't matter if it feels it. From start to finish, that's the way to do it, just like anything. Doing it without form and structure in between. In a sense forgetting what came before, but always offering a nod of recognition when it's called for. Keeping a flow, trying to establish a rhythm, a piece of existence, life, if you can call it that. Treating it with respect for as long as you can, until it drags and bleeds you.

The bottom fell out for all of us. The unions shrivelled up, workers accepted any condition: no benefits, no pay, no reality, just to keep their jobs and their minds. They became more obsessed with wage and saw themselves in growth – they felt like they were making progress at least.

I smoked the cigarette over by the window, watching the rain splash, dying for it to burn down and finish. It wouldn't smoke fast enough. The words were bubbling, I had to get them down. But the urge to stay by the window remained, the dimensions of the room closing in, the world edging out, words slipping down and away. The creative act was impure unless it was for someone else's benefit, and not just the self. I squandered the last bit of tobacco in the yellowed paper, dropping it out, running over to the bed.

For me, it hadn't gotten too much by then. But I was crumbling, ready to give in and never try again. I kept telling my self to relax, the pen still had the look of something meaningful and I was making progress, I thought. Soon I would have something down. I looked around the room and out the window with squinted eyes, satisfied. It was a world of grays that would soon get a shot of colour.

(EXT. BEDROOM - NIGHT)

I'd been reduced to this single room, a grubby little bedsit with cheap carpet spread everywhere. The stuff even ran along the walls, where it was beginning to peel off, and around the mirror where the moisture from the sink had made it mould and want to give way. The cigarettes made everything taste a little bitter, a little burnt, like the holes in my bed where I sat hunched over the reams of paper, setting in permanent back problems that would plague me for years to come, I was sure. It had already started to ache as I lay there twisted at night. Too many hours leaning over pages curled at the edges, too penniless to invest in a typer, or a chair, gripping my useless pen trying to make some sense.

No breakfast but a sachet of coffee I had managed to lift from a local cafe where I often had to go to shit when the communal toilet was backed up. The coffee powder sat like mud in the bottom of the cup where the water hadn't quite got hot enough in the kettle. Looking in there, at that brown smear, I realised I wasn't much, when I sat back and thought about the things I had done, trying so hard to be good and trustworthy and all those nice things mothers and fathers and bosses liked. Respectable. That was it. Something your neighbours would twitch the curtain to look at not because of the gaping walk that carried you over the pavement like some determined imbecile or because of the stained t-shirt and loosening trousers that fell so limp over your shoes, but because they knew your name, they recognised it on the post box and saw all the mail you were always getting and all the people that came to visit you in the evening and in the day and all the time. And what a happy man you must be and oh how they wished they had some of that happiness, and wouldn't it be nice to share a cup of coffee with him?

The world can disappear and reappear in a second.

Fools. I held to my self. My coffee tasted like dirt and I didn't have any milk. I never did. The fridge just rattled on empty like my sagging belly. And I laughed at them some more, that they had no clue all the letters falling out my box weren't friendly invitations or pithy little greetings from chums or even acquaintances, but rejections, not even proper correspondence, just slips saying *No we're sorry*, or *We're sorry to inform you that you'll never have a job here, you are pretty worthless, aren't you?* And the nights and the days weren't filled by knocks on the door from lovers, visitors and well-dressed companions but collectors, dealers and sometimes even worse, when I had the money. If they only knew how I skulked out my door, careful not to make a peep, slipping down the stairs to check for mail in the hope I had an acceptance letter, a job, a story, a poem, anything that would raise the spirits just a little, ease the pain for a moment. And all those other vices, I told my self they served a purpose. That I was an autodidact learning the twisted ways of the invisible world, making my self a seer. Turning my self inside and out wanting to understand, needing desperately to communicate discoveries to my fellow men. But it wasn't even that. It was a hunt for the wolf of acceptance.

In my most desperate hours I had even resorted to clasping my hands and praying to the God Almighty that he may save me from my misery, making deals with Him, promising I would serve him and believe in him if he made it happen, swearing I would go to church every day if he just gave me a blessing. A sign of hope. I sometimes found my self on my knees in the moisture, my sweaty hands glued together, mixing pinks and yellows and browns. Crying out, spittle around my lips as I spluttered promises to the air.

Robert Johnson bought the right idea. Anything to make it happen. Do what it takes. Kill the obsession with guilt and the others who have succeeded.

I smiled as a fine little hypocrite when the walls began to crumble.

(INT.)

Writing down everything you know is not the easiest thing you can think of. It can be slow. Rigorous. And you don't know what might become of it. Put simple, it's a test. A tedious one, I'd admit, but it'd be worth it anyhow.

Tingling chimes. The wind whistles, and I sleep. For days. The on. The off. Considering under closed curtains. Do. I. Need. It. I know that if I look back on that other life, some form of spirit will soak its way in. Some sign of achievement. Some dissolve of the embarrassment. And that might be my answer but to what I don't know yet. But she'd say, at least you're looking. And I was. I saw it once on some scribbled note pad that lay there untidy and needing clearing. And it picked me up and shone in my ear as I read it, as being something left bleeding, away from other eyes. There only for mine.

They say when the electric touches you, your breathing won't ever stop. And you'd lay awake immortal for all time in symbols to see.

So being truthful in all this—what putrid maelstrom of lies would allow their ageing to be tainted by fear for truth—the note, to my mind, made the hands the numbers. The faces falling off all the clocks. Well, it did for a minute anyway. If a minute's how you measure it. Thinking on it now, it's time itself and ageing that's dissolved the cells of thought that went before. All the pulsating lights, echoed sounds streaming on up the wrong way. Back into perception. That generation had already seen the 'too late' signs all over it. Intoxication. Mostly the depressants make it all seem a lot more 'real', to me anyway. I know someone who might agree. It was he that said it. But it's what he said after that caught me in the eye. And, well I don't know if me writing this makes it all real again. But maybe it's better said now rather than never. When my own voice will be heard out loud, and it won't be the loudest thing in my head anymore. My voice sounding through his. And the penny from heaven lands. Sent by the royal mint. Shaking the foundation of numbers all over. Maybe it's a race. Which external will win your mind outright? But you'll say, how am I the one to court such a judgment. For you or for me. Because when all the other questions have been answered, including maybe this, then this will have been one of those things said. But what can make me even certain of anything, this paper, the soaking ink, my hand and that light. And with the gavel's toll still ringing the litany in my ear, what am I doing and what have I done? Two completely unreliable things. But I can't admit to that. I've already seen it and known it too well.

Those were the moments that ever since have consumed my head and the worst parts of my soul. I'm going to be the first one to show out loud, the masks on all the ones like him. Where he goes now, doesn't matter. It'll never be safe again. He said it, and even then it was too late. I put it on account of a lot of things, mostly because I can't make up my mind. It doesn't have to be one thing anyhow, does it?

And last eternity wouldn't have been early enough for it to settle. But it's not me that makes those rules. Some think its all ego, others just part of it. A key in the door of the story. And that's odd. Most people make up their mind quick. Thinking nothing of it like it was too late by the time they'd done shut their mouths. Maybe even had it told for them. As it used to be. But the kids don't do shit. All that box. Them screens. All the natter, the in-turned face of regulation. Odious communication. And he proved it. Funny thing to me was: how he wasn't the first one to do it. Have the guts to throw it out there. But it was just at that time the rest of them had clicked on and that was what they were being told. I say the truth had never waited so long. But funny thing? When he says to me, sitting there face to face with me. One of us in shackles. The other fated for the jailhouse.

Was it worth it? There ain't no way we can stop it. It's been learnt. And they're all going to have to sleep on that, sighting at their tombstones. And that effrontery has yet to come crashing down. Still walking along that spider's web.

Because they ain't got no sense of humour.

It's the first thing you're told that makes you what you is. If it's gibberish. Then unlucky for you. If one sound bounces and really sponges that brain (and especially if it's repeated) then that's all you're going to be allowed to know. In those cubes. Squatting there, a load of us going crazy. Making it all happen from the inside out and then others watching. Just one. And another one dead. What you call that? Generation one?

I was lucky my word was Think. To begin with. But they showed me other words. And so on. This is where he garnered respect. And the timing. It shot all of everything to pieces, spread it out like a crazy woman's quilt, and it can't be repeated. Because thinking it and writing it once is enough. Clockwork, see.

Do we all have to be children? And so unprepared. Or have we got the final resolution in us.

They don't have to ask any more. He said. They won't have to. But that don't mean anything. It's just plain old comment. Doesn't mean anything. Something *vital* has to be said. To own it. To own the day and the night. And all that truth below until truth sits muddy in the sunken earth. Under wades of grass. Bringing down false notion and built-up depravity.

To let it die, the Old Man said. He taught me everything.

What a priggish fellow I was, worming around by day, then dipping seedily into the undergrowth by night. Anything to force out some material. Anything would do, but just sitting and breathing wasn't enough sometimes. How terribly they would all judge me if they knew what I was up to as they slept cosily in their beds by TV-light, some incessant chatter coming out at them through plasma rays. I often thought the landlady a victim of minor brain damage. What else could come of her eyes constantly flickering before that screen. That hag from Swansea. A soft beard emerging from her chin. A little lady who took pleasure threatening me through the walls, banging it when I refused to open the door, just to put the fear into me. So I'd fill the lock with a piece of old cardboard so her key couldn't fit. Whenever she came for the rent I just sat in silence not moving, pretending to be out. I had often waited for anything up to three hours before risking any movement. The building so old it would give me away.

She usually settled down and left for the shops, as she did every day, with her thick scarf and long coat buttoned to her neck, waddling along and out the gate, always returning with all manner of useless tat.

She had gotten into the habit of slamming on my door as she walked past, or giving it a swift little kick. I had seen her do it from the stairway as I returned one day, hiding in the alcove careful for her not to sense my presence. But now, the old avoidance game was growing a little repetitive. I knew I would have to do something about the rent soon. I smoked the rest of my cigarettes as I tried to fix the kettle. Thinking on my problems, I worked the spoon around the edges of the cup, scraping the remaining granules into the lukewarm water. The taste of dirt mixed with my ashen stomach caused the familiar heaves. I vomited weak yellowy bile into the sink.

I sat back on the bed and I looked out the window where all the greys began to wash over me.

They just shrugged and looked right back.

CHAPTER TEN

I awoke the next morning with the burning sensation at the back of my throat. It had a unique flavour and was tangy like a cough drop. I began to suck at the sides of my mouth and lick my gums for the taste. I spat out the rest in the sink and watched the thick phlegm covering the plughole. It just sat there. I ran over to my papers and scribbled what I was feeling.

It was all tedious, of course. Feeling then translating, having to use representations of notions, of concepts, then attempting communication through the network of language set for me, without my consent. It was certainly tedious, if not completely futile. I wanted to just reach out and touch something. I watched my self all feverish, like a boy trying to succeed at a man's game. So I ran out the door and down the stairs out to some indiffer-ent clouds that had just began to down with rain. I saw my self running along, running at speed trying to live, running at life trying not to rhyme words in my head. My feet stung as they hit the hard stone beneath, holes in my shoes getting to be all around the sole, feeling as if I was running bare foot. The rain began to gush as I hit along the road, everyone else was scattering around me, panicking for the weather's sudden turn. I jetted past umbrellas and monochromatic people, all the suits and fashionable clothing that I wondered at. How the fashions had changed and how they would change again, and all those people were going to feel foolish in not so long because their photographs will reveal to them what silly followers they were. I giggled and leapt, glad in my skin and delighted with my ragged clothing until I caught a glimpse of my discoloured body in the window of a restaurant.

And I stopped.

I stared, as I seemed to have a habit of doing then. Inside I saw my self, sipping hot coffee and toasting the day's blessings with fellow worker-ants and biting juicy bacon sandwiches, dripping with brown sauce, crunching with crispy fats. I imagined my self looking healthy, over-fed and delighted. No more pains through that window, I thought.

The words of the menu burst out and punched me in the stomach.

Soaked and defeated I gazed on through the window until I saw my self from the other side.

A portrait of agony standing limp in the rain, dripping from all the sharp corners of my bones. I pondered that sight of a man so broken and so beat, so helpless in his insanity, who had moments ago been bounding along the street giggling with manic indignation.

I was learning something.

This new knowledge soaked me like the rain, every new thought hit me with blunt force. The world faded behind me and my vision grew strong, not in what I was seeing, but in what I realised I was now supposed to do. I was to leave this place and step out onto the wild urban trail. I had to quit my apartment building and survive alone amongst the wilderness, the wilderness of the city.

No more attachments, no more things or possessions. Perhaps just a pen, some paper and packfuls of stolen cigarettes. Of course, it wasn't for any political motive or deluded reasoning like that. Just me, the pretension and the cold, cold lonely street.

I looked up and around, at all the automatons scuttling under the safety of shelter, screaming inside with such disdain for nature, as I thought noble thoughts of one day explaining their world to them.

I thanked the gushing heavens for the opportunity and I let the earth take hold.

CHAPTER ELEVEN

I was never any good at being discrete. My words shot loud and quiet in an uneven jamboree. There's no need for the consistent voice. Only dead men speak with consistent tongues. And I always found it more effective to just stay still, curl up into a heap if threatened. Cowards often win the day and inherit vast fortunes this way. So when I reached the top of the stairs, finally ready to ditch the bedsit and abandon my rent problem, I wasn't sure if it was some powerful hallucination that had taken hold, but the sight made me reel back and put my hands over my head as if something was about to strike my skull.

I peeped through my fingers to take another look. My room door was ajar. I could feel the breeze of the open window coming through. I pushed it gently, the hinges creaked and shook where they had been loosened. I took it all in at once.

The carpet had been stripped from the floor and the walls. Filth and old washing-up was strewn about, and not all of it mine. Water had been poured across the floor in a haphazard manner, and there was a faint smell of petroleum shifting about the place. The window sat open as if apologetic for what it had witnessed and had been powerless to stop.

We had been ransacked. My papers wept half-torn around the room, and in the sink more of them lay soaking in the phlegm. The mattress was up against the wall and my stash of tobacco gone. The wall by the window dripped with rain blown inward.

Everything squelched as I inspected it, assessing the damage. The kettle was filled with more of my papers and was still on when I got to it, warming them gently. I took it all as I sign I was no longer welcome.

Probably just the landlady having a bit of a fit, I supposed to my self, no point worrying about such trivial issues, I was glad that I had made my solemn vow earlier and took the whole episode as serendipitous. I must admit, I was a little surprised there was nothing from the landlady, a little profanity scrawled on a note perhaps, or a vague threat on my life written in blood across the carpet walls. She was quite capable of all of this I was certain, but she probably didn't want to damage her own property any further, I had decided. But to expect I would still live there after all this? Ha, she really was a dunce.

Good then, I thought, time to mosey on out. The world for a pauper is a beautiful one if he understands that he is truly rich, not just in that grand sense, which is really a lie, such as the pretension of riches in liberty and adventure, free to explore and reconcile all the differences he has come to understand, but wealthy in such a way that he begins to unlearn all of the things that previously gripped him.

He starts a new life, a fresh existence that can feed his Being sufficiently, by casting aside all the false notions, the whispers that echoed dizzy in his head before. He has the time for reflection firstly, and if he takes the opportunity, he has the time to begin to understand the way things *are* rather than how they *should* be. In this he'll feel rich for a while, at least, and until the meaning of his position becomes a burden upon his shoulders; he can be free of all the inculcations that subdue mankind in every manner of speaking. He will at times feel utterly strong with real force and power, over himself and his perceptions, and ultimately over the way he utilises his waking life. He will transcend his manufactured needs and exist for a new understanding, and this will make him indestructible. Immortal before death. He will last out through the ages until the earth falls beneath him and gives way to a new laugh. And these men exist, always will, as long as the earth is not overrun by some grave catastrophe.

I sloped down the stairs pondering my grand ideas, that maybe I could be the man I spoke of, the rich pauper. And as I stepped out of the building I had never felt such a divine hope rise up and protect me. I was awakening to the world and its ways. Alcohol and amphetamines would be a thing of the past. All vices cast out. No more saturnine afflictions. The walls must stop moving of their own accord. I would no longer choose the pot or the whiskey, or the pill and the quick, quick bottle.

My thoughts were greeted by the clouds. They mustered a familiar countenance and ushered me forth with an eagerness to hold me. They were no longer indifferent to my plight; they would be my podium for all the great promises to come. Upon the new life I was shaping, a new philosophy would be born, a way out for all the stolen people and all their stolen minds. For them, things were going to be changed forever, and they would understand everything and the world within.

(INT.)

Some nomads, all they have is the road. Nothing to move forward on, to assault. Just open gravel in the pit. Some have even less. They are dying, or dead. Some have little more.

We are already dead.

The road laid out in front, each step of each journey meaning less distance to some ultimate judgement. The ones awake to this know, they know well. They have no need for tour guides or sponsors. Their mind is the only tour possible. They have no use for maps, must-see sights or destinations. They only need one map and it is not written down on any page. Their destination: none. Just several more steps before there are no more the muscles can take.

On their map, the contours are flat. Mountains collide with the crawling city. The sea, the beach, the ocean: on top of caves, in the mouth of the carnival. Reason and hope do not stand or figure. There are no calculations. The words they speak have viscous vagueness. The man, the hitcher, has no words, numbers or ideas to explain. Justification is pointless but he wants you to work that out for yourself. He does not question you. He expects no answers. He only talks with you, laughing at the ironies, the paradox, the nature and the way of some Thing. These thoughts can fill his day. It may be the same the next, or it may be different. The difference is, it does not matter. He does not clutch at the straws of fulfilment, or any resolution in complete tourism.

He may speak no language. He rarely writes things down. He decides for himself and accepts no responsibility apart from himself.

He may have belongings or he may not, but if he does they will be few and make little sense to anyone but him. He may have the clouds in his eyes. He may have sunshine between his toes. He spits in guidebooks and seals the pages. He has many concerns but none of them matter much to him. He always carries water. He frequently gives his pocket and hand to strangers. He has no prejudice. Often he just stands still.

He never has to look through a window because he is never found behind one. He has no profound principles or roll of ethics; he does not preach, judge, expect or demand. He sees a car crash every day. He sees a thing die every day. He sometimes sees new things born.

He plays by the string and knows his way might be wrong.

He does not search for completeness, although if he found it he says he would not recognise any part of it.

He often sits for days because he cannot live forever.

He does not die. And he may already be dead.

He does not compete.

It is all equal.

Mental images, as digital records, are without feeling or meaning. The past has shown me real experience is in no way aided by the dead capturing of straw buildings. Some fountain in the centre of a square. Immovable symbols of freedom amongst drenched commerce. The tourist and his camera, eager and misinformed. Stealing moments to store on some memory disk. Camera flashes just like the collective amnesia of those that visit. So momentary and fleeting. Repeated clutching. The photo album is filled with death – nothing captured, no flavour, no picture, no breath. Disposable imagery snapped and stored but hardly recalled. Imposed values of their minds cannot escape the futility of pressing buttons. They do not realise, interest in these things is severely limited when a rectangular shape is filled with some abstract thing far away and with only the most fleeting meaning. They are like sunburn. Or wandering free-range chickens. Bobbing on hind legs, snapping with featherless wings at anyone present and anything in their line of sight. Day-sack adage, flopping sandals. Look at the stern, robotic faces instead. The armed guards and steel eyes. The street sweeper amongst it every day. Employed and needed by the limited conversation and tourism of these amateurs. It's a waste, but self-righteousness is not, to them. As hungry as the pigeons and just as lost and pointless.

The many pains I felt stemmed from a growing respect for desperation.

People flocking like birds. Vultures waiting on street corners. The pack of hyena.

(EXT. STREET - DAY)

As I glided down the path beset by riches of lush trees and brightly coloured flowers, I spread my arms and reached out my hands as if to welcome the new understanding. I closed my eyes and angled my face to the sun. I breathed in heavily and received a welcome in return. The air was crisp. It had never been so clean. It rushed up my nose and around my body like a spirit in a new dimension. It was the universal understanding, and it lifted me up, up, up.

I felt a surge of energy; I had to be with more of this sublime nature. I became cretinous for it, a fiend for the universe. I began to stride with long steps. My eyes still closed, I felt every slap of my shoe not with pain, but complete and utter joy.

A mass of ideas began to present themselves on my mind's page. A hundred ways to start a new story: There is no ship now that can bury me yet. All the majesty and all the prose stampeding together. Drifting lines of poetry, oozing out life into one another as if delicately assembled by subconscious magic hidden from me. Sympathetic strings for sympathetic hearts. They all began to reverberate through my fingers as I waltzed along, past the restaurant now forgotten, past all the shop windows and porcelain-faced women, their flaccid eyeballs straining to understand.

I was free at last.

The slow years of failure beginning to dissolve, tears all forgotten. Embarrassment set aside.

I was climbing up the shit heap to something built in the sky. Even clichés seemed bright and memorable. It was all coming together.

In times of turning through torrid skies and leaning on wheels of chrome to shaken tones of clean neckties and stale upstarts, pointed down quarks with tootsie roll parts...

The lad, his chasing laces kicking angrily but obediently behind, rips the pavements up as his scurry grows more desperate and shuddered. Following. Thinking: there is some way to lead here, some path to show. If only these stolen shoes could make more burning sacrifices to the idols I worship. To that dead end I chase like the hungry mongrel waiting impatiently for the final purge, every meal consciously his last.

And instead of turning about, looking these towers of

gold up and down, the fleeting currencies that bear hor-
rendous burdens and thinking of what paper, the paper
of books, that holds real value, the only currency worth
printing are in those pages of type. Concentrated texts
that now crumble and yellow over the epochs – where
amongst the dust new weeds will emerge – all this, but
instead I plunder on, tumbling and flailing down the
snowy mountainside – spitting tame limericks, lame
jokes – (and pausing for applause) – tumbling... tumbling... a metaphor for my own existence. All of this,
this suckling from the teet of group respiration. Needing
some feeling of worth from ugly pedantry. I never look
back at my self because the pain would be shattering. So
my shoelaces stay untied, my feet stumbling forth and
pointedly inwards, my head down, watching the scent.
Never letting it escape. And I realise what I have lost, but
it doesn't occur I can get it back by ending this carnival
show of existence, toying with ego, moulding shapes and
fantasies with ego play-doh. Realising, I am not this and
I am not real, I have no value and my mockery to genius
is my delusion of impending greatness. I thought of the
burnt reams left behind by incisive minds. Lifetimes of
work bitten by the dust.

　　I need to sit in the grass somewhere, lean against some
omniscient tree, let its aching branches crumble around
me and swallow me down to the core of the flats, the reality, the dream. My self-righteousness is some power in

itself. Preying on those I see as weak, where the lad, I, was once the morally bullied. I now become the dominator, the wraith, the wrath and the scourge. Of ethical watch-towers. And this power flies through me and lifts all of this essence, everything I feel. I no longer have fleets of doubt waiting to set sail. My self-certain, self-righteousness is some blunder I have not yet recognised. So I chop down the mountain - the Axe in my hand - step on its broken neck and pound the abdomen with balled fists. It is bitterness, anger. All raging hatred, red and painful, screaming to non-existent figures about and above me, believing the word 'special' worst of all.

I believe I will live on through some magnum opus. And ultimately, I think I am immortal.

I dipped in my pocket for my pen to take hold of this terrific epiphany. I put the dry tip on the curve of my tongue. I wouldn't have to use this old pen and paper for long, I smiled to my self. A typewriter, perhaps an apartment, an office, a wall of books and ideas and references. A glass ceiling. All that knowledge I would have at my fingertips.

I beamed at the world and it beamed back.

We were partners again.

CHAPTER TWELVE

Two weeks had passed. Glorious weeks of sheer productivity like I had never experienced before. No more purposely alienating prose. Who would have known the will to power lay dormant within me all this time. Only I. And it didn't matter where I was sitting, inspiration met me at every turn. I hadn't stopped writing but to chat a little here and there, steal some paper and snack down now and then, only when the hunger struck. Hunger that would only dig in its heel when the brakes were pressed.

I had worked out a tight little system. Any beggar of a romantic disposition would have been proud. I sat on benches out in the open, main roads mostly, busy places where the buzz of life and history shivered through my pen. When my pits and feet began with the stink, I walked over to the National History Museum not too far off. I tidied my self up a little, straightened my back and wore a studious expression. Real serious and puzzled, about problems of quantum physics and bosons and quarks and up down strange, all that. I wiped my hair into a side parting, greased and flat. I walked on in and kept the quizzical expression as I passed by security, throwing out a 'hmm' now and then, or touching my chin with my thumb and index finger. I just needed to look clean enough to get in and get to the bathroom.

I buttoned up my coat to the neck to cover my shabby attire. It was long enough, down to the shins, to cause a distraction from my shoes, just enough to get by. I always thought it was the smell that gave me away, so I often dropped into a supermarket where security was always most lax to spray a little deodorant under my pits, a little on my groin where I thought most of the odour derived from. Occasionally I dipped my hand into a pot of gel and arranged my hair in a fashionable way, spread a little aftershave here and there, then was on my way. It always did the trick for the museum security. I got to the bathroom for a quick wash up, a tidy little standing shower.

That was only until I came upon the undiscovered treasure of the polytechnic university situated near the main railway station. There they had zero security. Inside were these cubicles for religious students, equipped with showerheads for washing the anus. I felt a little horrid going in there, the state I was in, but it was a revelation for me. I washed every few days to keep the stench at bay and was often clean. I felt a little guilty when I saw someone enter the toilet after I had just taken advantage of it: it's a personal thing going to the toilet and I felt a little lousy having to take such measures. The guilt followed me only until I reached the main hub of student activity, the quadrant. I overheard conversations, meaningless chatter in high pitched voices compelled to finish with the AQI, beeping about shoes on shelves and photographs on the Internet, and where did they get them? There's a picture on the Internet? And ow, how it hurts to hear. They were usually quite generous with their smokes though, only giving a furtive raised eyebrow to their friends, which meant nothing to me, I can assure you.

The convenient discovery of the university library also meant I would no longer have to walk into office buildings pretending to work there and steal paper from the copying machines, walking out with the fear I was being followed and watched. Always followed and watched by the tightly dressed demons. I could go into the library, even sleep a wink during twenty-four hour opening times, and take paper as and when it was required, read their books for nothing and keep warm as I worked. Quite a few discoveries in two weeks, I felt.

Yet the lingering expectance of something horrific crawling over the white horizon grew and grew inside, it hadn't gone so well for this long ever before. I had even begun to consider self-publishing, and by hand, I assumed at little to no cost, distributing around the English department. But overhearing their conversations I thought it would be a waste. They wouldn't understand the isolation and humiliation, not yet at least. They all had places to go home to, and people to see, and beer to drink and whatnot. In a few years their studies would be faint memories like a raising mist, and they would brandish their knuckles and put them down. Their three years a mere rite of passage.

I had begun to think that writing wasn't about the inspiration; it wasn't really even about the words. If some of those people on the shelves hadn't had these lives, soaked in alcohol and abuse and dusted with all kinds of little helpers and devils along the way, would they even be there? Or just dead and forgotten in the gutter.

If they didn't have the dominating culture behind them, the foundation that supported all the bullshit that the occidental wall had constructed over the years, ignoring all the magic in the closed-up mouse holes, would they even be there? Maybe the mouse holes were imaginary. Maybe there was no hidden talent. Maybe some of them didn't even want to write, only to become the creator rather than consumer. Or they just wanted to better understand what they read, or to at least talk about it like they did. Like me, I found my self starving to understand. Any type of madness inflicted upon the self to alter perception. Take advantage of the experience and filter it out into something new. Surrounded by structures made by man, to feed man, like the restaurants that hang dead cooked animals in the window, or stack piles of bread up to the ceiling made for you to ache.

I would find my self holding back temptation to try and understand the ones that had gone before me. Drooping eyes that perused the delicacies on display, licking the inside of my mouth and imagining the satisfactory taste of it all. I would keep promising my self a big hefty meal at the end of the day, something to sleep on and not wake up hungry, after all I had quite a bit of money stashed in the inside pocket of my coat, money that I'd held back from the landlady. I just chose not to share it.

I drank water from the drinking fountain when I felt the sanity slipping, or when the vocabulary started to stiffen. The most infuriating was when the spelling went, that was when I really panicked and started to think I was losing any mental faculties I may have had. Still clinging to old ideas I thought, that was what was holding me back. I wouldn't self-publish, what good would it do. It was all shit anyway. Nothing I had written, all those bloodless lines of poetry, all those stories about nothing trying to be about everything.

(INT.)

He sits cross-legged, leaning forward over his lap. The sunlight shines from the page to his wandering imagination eagerly flicking pictures, words, in his own language. His eyes blinking larger in awe and eager hope. In a room, in a block, in an estate where the middle class are the residents. Some mix-up there. And although the hammer and the sickle hang in close memory, the ideals slice through lives and are laid near ground. Ceviche emotions raw and juicy held back by the universal idea of money, currency and value. Worth. Accepted class-barriers sitting on cushioned armchairs, rested on laurels. Slow campfire desire like a stolen look across a licking flame. Moments flying like flakes of ash from the pit. In the morning that campfire may still be glowing. Or quenched. Ashen remnants.

The land is dark. All across it the soldier ant scampers to the beat of deceit. The rebel looking out double-glazed windows, earth quaking white, squalor of foetuses on street corners rock and sniff. Flashing violent and abrupt inhalations and numbness of snotty noses. Television flickers.

One white bar. Two white bars, more. Then no picture, no lights, no hum. Laughter, crying, baiting, resting. All a tease. Silenced. The pueblo are looking up. Around. Darting and useless. Minions and pawns among us. I hear the birds. They are not singing. The ground shook, rumbling beneath like it was all caving in for the end. Whimpers and shouts mixed across the verve. Glass rattling, china, plates, all of it quivering to some carnal screams.

I heard the hundreds of doors swinging and slamming open, timid fear. Some profound silence followed for some time, whispers only. Inquisitive conspiring, some expected panic. Those sleeping in beds are now deaf to shooting and silent murder. Their oil is spent and chickens cluck on. Not on civil war. I looked at the other brash gleam in the room, away in the corner. Consideration imminent. My weeping neighbours. Some of the fallen. Screams in far, far away places – primal and desperate. Using all of the lung and the heart, every drop of blood rising and resounding. Human sirens. The pressure had dropped. Hills and perception torn apart.

A man in a porch, smoking. A wife dyeing her hair. A song. Holding dirty dishes. The girl pattering in the street. An army of insects rushing in one direction. The Bomb had ended that and now you have to ask the unpaid chimes of revolt.

The barrel tasted like a penny. Like metallic blood. Or sucking on a tingling battery. The power was out now and only glimmers of light confounded the matte darkness.

The final equation my pistol solved was the one in my head. And it came like the Rapture.

Falling pylons. Gunning myself in the head.

I keep dreaming of earthquakes. Violent and fierce.

State violence, law. The individual's, a crime.

(EXT. LIBRARY - NIGHT)

It didn't take much longer before I went back to whimpering in the corner of the third floor, by the sociology section, starving and pathetic. There is a scent that haunts me. At select moments it wafts in from some grave place and filters up my nostrils. It is her smell. The one that will never be forgotten. And it always takes me away to some place chained and dead.

I ate my bread roll, my meal for the day, taken from the canteen where the cooks don't look, thinking of the others who had to do the same, telling my self always that I'd get a hot meal when dusk set. How those words soothed me: hot meal. A lightness in the chest. But I had begun to sob when I read back the first things I had written on that day I was ransacked. Now a tightness in the chest. It was the most mediocre garbage I had ever written. No, ever seen. It was completely beyond me. I held it taut in my hands as I read each creeping word. How could it be? I spat on the page and had to throw it out the window. Words of cloying desperation, complete obsession with eschatology and prediction, and when it might come and how it might look with all the reds and the oranges and the yellows and the burning flames rising out of the torn sky, the earth laid scorched and lifeless beneath. Or why was it always fire that I had in my head, why not the land, a green paradise lively and swaying in the wind, a house on the hill and laughter all around, water flowing in a stream along a bank, the sun white and watching down. Why? Because it is more disturbing. Far more regrettable.

Then a blink. A blink. And death laid evenly across the landscape. For all of time.

All right there, Joe?

He came bounding at me with a broad streak of yellow and brown teeth smeared across his chin. He sat on a bench one away. Then got up and sat a couple seats from me at the end of mine.

Everything all right there, Joe?

Yeah, yeah. He said.

Good?

Yeah yeah.

He was in the other place, smiling and giggling to himself as he sat flicking lint off his dirtied knees and looking up and smiling again and shaking his head a little to the side as if to say: I can't believe it.

What are you so giddy about?

Ah nothin'. Just a bit of joy in this dark place, isn't there? He turned to look at me.

Why, what's happened?

Nothin', nothin'. He skipped around the question mark and continued to chuckle a little and turn and look up at me, then the sky.

Go on. What is it? I tried to wrench it out of him. The bastard had something and he wasn't telling.

Nothin' there, buddy. I'll catch ya later.

Wait. I said.

He was gone, walked off out of the park, hands in the pockets, still shaking his head and laughing.

CHAPTER THIRTEEN

(INT.)

The days rolled on, and I struggled through them, scrounging for immortality in work. I could stare at brick walls for hours, all manner of images feasting on my brain and my eyes. Apophenia could cloud days of my life at a time. As I walked down the street, the pareidolic faces of buildings smiled or guffawed or stood astonished. Faces were leaning out at me from everything. I knew what was real though, at least I had that on them.

I found one brick wall, near where I had found Joe. There was a freshly painted black bench in front of it. Some memorial to a couple who had died together, three days apart according to the placard. I sat down as the cold wind took up the corner of my coat, parting my hair with a heavy gust. I squinted my eyes, shielding them from the harsh winter air. As I squinted, the colours of the wall accentuated, individual bricks joined with others and formed images, visions uncontrollable.

On the wall stood a figure I recognised as my self. I was in a different coat, yet still long and black, but the wind made no matter of it – it blew just as hard as it did sitting there. I was walking somewhere. I looked closer at my eyes, squinting them further together. I could make out the tears streaming down my cheeks, blown to my ears by the shooting winds. I sobbed and fought the wind, battling through it to get somewhere. Then it faded and refreshed anew.

Words flashed on new images.

The dogs rule the night. Silently hunting through dim streets, surrounding territories in small-knit packs. I ran, paranoid. The watchdogs sleep dead on junctions awaiting all comers. Alerts patrol crossings and corners, panting at the sight of an outsider, a portion of meat. Dogs of prey venting through all open space. Yet they do not paste propaganda on the walls, on the floors, or even need to.

Wilderness can reign a part of anything. And raw teeth and anger stand on four stalking legs, mastering the science of fear by having none and thinking less. Primal instincts awakened at sundown and siesta.

The town open to rampage, a slow rumbling.

And we are all dying. For some it will come soon. For others, not soon enough.

But for now they can't claim the days. And we wait.

I begin again. Write.

He had been out of the loop for way too long. He

hadn't even noticed the horrors going on around. He may have spotted it once, outside the library, near the beginning of those first days. The new organisation. They wore badges that read: Metro Polis. It was spreading, he saw it plastered on the chests of those that passed by from time to time, when he was out in the wobbling street. He thought at first they must have been officials, journalists, and so on, they had notepads out and were taking information, striking a balance between Polis and journalists, both out on the road, both taking down selective information, both reporting, though different in class, to a higher authority.

They dressed all in black and wore heavy stares that buckled the interviewees, making them helpless under the tirade. He must have been on the way to visit the Old Man, he had a bag with him, and a swollen throat.

The world's an evil place without breakfast. How 'bout a drink?

And a think.

OK. I won't talk.

The barman walked off.

I wasn't one for status. The only label I needed was the Black one.

We sat at the bar. All of us heroes. Heroes of circum-

stance, victims of will.

Large Johnnie Walkin'.

Same for me. Iced.

I grunted. Let it get cold, pulled the cubes out of the glass and slapped them on the bar, most of the blocks falling at my feet.

Slammin 'em down in a podunk bar like this never seemed a good idea, but at least amusing.

Large Johnnie Runnin'.

I ordered another.

Was bout to be another monochromatic day in the hinterlands.

Who are you? I asked.

PART FOUR

Iris In

Black

CHAPTER ONE

I was running when I got to the door. Slow death.

It was locked. I peered in, not too concerned. Most of my panic was out of the way quick, and now that the usual slow ebb of anxiety was leaving me, I fumbled the keys into their locks with the realisation that I have nothing, only a no-body, waiting in that room.

I almost didn't want to go back in now. I decided that I shouldn't. Before I was up the wide spiralling staircase I smelt tobacco smoke oozing gently round the building. It was comfort enough that all was right in the pit. I tiptoed away and down the stairs, leaving the tenement door ajar.

He watched from a distance. They spoke only in bursts, quick questions with faces expecting answers. They stood in front of a group of youngsters. The crowd cowered at their presence, but some seemed more than happy to help. They pointed around, tracking the invisibles that must have committed some kind of reportable transgression. Metro Polis nodded, taking more notes.

One spoke into a walkie-talkie; the other edged away to leave. They signalled to an unknown power, got into a small black car without gesturing a thanks or goodbye and left, sitting rigid and facing ahead. The car slipped away down the road as clouds began to march.

He went on down the side roads, to the Old Man, with thoughts of fear in his head and dread in his stomach. It wasn't strange to him that the authorities would be investigating something outside that building, heavy activity there, hand-to-hand business and the like. But their body language instilled something in him. Looking up at the marching clouds seemed appropriate.

It had been months since the last visit to the Old Man in the high rise. 11th floor. Wait for the lift. Step in. Some youths had decided it appropriate to spray something incoherent on the inside of the carriage. The word BEAT may or may not have been in there, it was hard to tell. But it looked as if someone had tried to set fire to the elevator on one side the way the black spray curling around from one corner to another. The anxiety grumbled.

Devil's template.

An even gore cleaning the streets whilst palladiums of people chase across vast planes, fleeing dusty ruins.

Wilderness can rule a part of anything.

Once heaving beds now lay prey to any creature above and below the green. Dressed in muddy dearth, the rapine laid across the land to claim souls and leave absolutely soiled and desolate remains – of thought and feeling. Go somewhere.

Hollow carcasses staring up and everywhere, obeying the futility of their exodus. See them. Made prone and immovable by blunt manifestoes of hateful and intelligent machinery, eternally instilled in the cavernous vessel that is the automaton's function. Turn it inside. An acerbic monstrosity of mechanic instruction fermenting to be injected into the bloodstream. A bane to the innocents. Indiscriminate destruction by everything presumptuous enough to rest their fingers on the trigger and let the heat loose, on towns and all of quivering civilisation. Watch it. The pacifist sweats drunk in the puddle above the drain, getting sucked down by a gentle current, but he is too wide to slip down into the sewer underground. Change it. The man with the determined bones holds the chamber to his skull, crooked and helpless, shot in the mind but still responsive. Reactive. Murderous with loathing. At peace with the flow.

But first he thoroughly digs his own grave and begins to rot his flesh. The soul, in its servility to the body, catalyses the process and prepares for struggle. Slowly preparing for judgement.

And worried about originality.

He spoke as he entered the corridor. The white hall whispered. The walls dripped yellows and browns; bulbs flickered above from the near-defunct lighting. He breathed, heaving slightly, then released a watery substance like an overflowing pipe. The rain had begun to fall against the building, the fresh odour mixing through the window behind him, and he felt he was a part of it. He stumbled forward, still dribbling, through to the end door. Flat 1117. A knock.

From the other side the Old Man rose from his chair, lightly cursing his cracked knees. The Old Man moved across the room, the window letting in some dreary yellow sun through the brown curtains on the far side of the room. He had been sitting in the kitchen of the open-planned apartment. The flies circulated his head as he walked, he shifted slowly past the couch, his chair, all the necessary furniture that seemed to have materialised itself over the years, things he could have easily pushed out the window to send dripping down to the concrete below. It was concrete above, too. It was concrete everywhere. He cursed his knees again as he reached for the lock. Concrete knees too.

The Door opened.

The Old Man spoke. Your happiness is equal to your ignorance. Look at you, you look like sewer scum and headed for a breakdown.

There is no win or lose; it's not a game. The young man replied.

The Old Man scrunched his face in disbelief. Listen to you, who do you think you're impersonating? The Old

Man shuffled his feet to the side of the opening, allowing the darkened figure through.

The door opened fully. Come on then, he says, come in and wipe your mouth.

Thanks, he whispered. What was his name anyway? Something twitchy, weak and malleable. Come to that later.

Sit down.

He sat for a moment feeling, and probably looking, quite baffled in the back of his chair, looking in the mirror across the room.

Contemplation is a sport. Never forfeit, but know there is no outcome. They had started their game at the door, and now it continued within: they uttered platitudes and clichés at each other, confounding each other with phrases of absurdity and meaninglessness.

Good start today, he thought. These words, he supposed, were wisdom, even revelation, to some. Those that considered the word 'deep' as appropriate to their vocabulary of what it meant to think for oneself. You're deep, man. Ha. He told the Old Man about this. But confused through concentration, he could barely feel himself, and the words he wanted to play next evaded his lips.

He wanted to get out of the seat, spit out something again.

Eternity and identity have played together for too

long in our hearts. We leave no time to step back and watch from some tower over the city.

Maybe we're feeling too immersed.

They laughed.

I took another hit of air and became my self again: Maybe you're right, though.

I looked at what he had been writing:

I am all. I am everything, turning to nothing. I am free. I am shackled. I am that. I am no other.

I can't believe you didn't play these.

Too obvious. So what've we got today? We can finish our game later.

Quickly and sharply, unbeknownst to the Old Man, a pounding and rumbling were hailing up the stairway. The stairway shot black and chrome with steel. Heavy uniforms flashing through. Walkie-talking boldly into radios and thunder in bullet-proof armoury.

They had finally come for him and I thought: I deserved to go too. No, it was just paranoia. There was nothing out there. Calm down. That doesn't lead anywhere.

I was being floated down the staircase. My arm throws an impotent hook, as if through water in a dream. Lazy. Slow.

The chrome swallowed in my thoughts; speeding grass re-coloured all the life around me as it blurred past each leaping bound I let out. Dogs barked, like they do.

People stared, as they have done. And the light vanished when I had made it back to the security of the old interior.

Hungry I thought. I breathed again. Knee deep in the asylum.

Want to eat something? The Old Man asked.

Maybe later, I don't know if I can hold anything down.

Well, there's soup in the pot if you want something. The Old Man ran his fingers over the wooden veneer of his desk. Have you got anything for me? Got a lot on at the moment actually, need something to keep it going.

The end of antique. I announced. How about it?

Yes, sure. Hum. What is it?

Just a little yum-yum. Here, have a look for yourself.

I handed over the packages from his sack.

They look a little yellow. The Old Man fingered the shapes.

Yeah, they'll make you that way too.

Go on then, how much?

Well, Gramps, for you. Resume the game and I'll think about it.

The Old Man chuckled through his bristled cheeks. Their game continued, the elder reciting from his Formica heart:

Rarely is it mentioned and perhaps rarely is it considered, the pungency of the decay. Things on hills, people in cities, what we stand on: decaying. The slow rot of prin-

ciples that existed before, amalgams of new ideas, but all of it part of some false exploit and control of wilderness. Whilst, out there somewhere, human wildebeest still reign God and country for their own prowess living with no servility but only to the drumming servitude of time... circumstance... and space. No strolling introductions but the recognition of primitive ability and forgotten natural instinct. Never omitting lives to complete McGuffin existence. Found in the lost bins, recovered for always. Have you seen them run, lost, across moors spanning entire continents? Chased by hungry engines throttled in harboured chests? Instead, in walls of crumbling gray and muck-stained gardens, thousands multiply the end. Pills as meals and spit for hydration. Choking on gambit that will die easy, because lies die that way. And so the traveller thinks, sitting in blue gloom. Missing home from the Black Flag party on television. Why is it that some have moved completely against the idea of travel? One place, one mind, analysing closed society. The nature of this place. The mass for voice-over actors.

They laughed again.

You deserve it, no charge, the young man said to the old.

He came back with his own.

We can breathe for

Taking motion and barbaric reaction,

From currency insistent gods while

They take your hand and the
Monetary values in their inconsistently
Flowered fires, bouncing within atmospheres
Of tense shoulders, diving blades and
Shaken heart,
Until
Clicking fingers set some pace, impatient
Adultery of worn faith, hollowed in shrunken belief.

A retort from the Old Man burst forth through stifled laughter as soon as I'd uttered my last word: *On solid
temptations. These things don't crumble, only circle what
can be had and ending all that can afford to be stolen or
bought with dirt. Slow. Crossing legs and battling minds
that hold fort in the walls of strange crews, held underneath by failing vines strewn 'round natural pools, over
rotten pains and stung, drawn pins. Nothing above that
great mass, that towering nimbus that falls on the heads
and aching necks of those holding aspiration or attempts
to retract old habits from new hierarchies.*

*They can write it down, across, so it is not all forgot-
ten, but spelling is not their strongest suit. So sitting on
the floor is a nuisance, and having little else to measure,
apart from the numbers of clenched fists, their struggle
will be up and down to the knees that faltered, giving way
to fungal essence. What else can be had from swirling ego
in misty whirlpools? Evil left as moisture un-evaporated,
crystal remnants dusting from shuddering towers of an-*

ger, the accused can return to familiar tables but sit in silence of the lonely wrath. Aborted pains from private doorways. Persistent quakes and safety sought in minimal solitude. Weakened joints on shacks and bookshelves that house little but the memory of sacrifices. Before the purge. Before the rapture. And only when it's all burnt, and only then, can you explore the shapeless ash.

That's a winner, we both decided. You wrote that earlier. I can tell.

Did not, protested the Old Man in petty reticence, as they both moved toward the near-opaque windows.

Say it plainly. The Old Man said. Let our game absolve all the bullshit from you. Use up all the pretension. Spend it unwisely. Together we can get through the muck.

Yes. Terse. We looked out the window. It's hard to get it all out when it festers and keeps building. No matter how much of it I spew, more wants to be written.

The Old Man stood back and watched him. Don't I know it. He said. I remember the bestseller lists. But keep trying. He rested his hand on the young man's shoulder.

We stood for a moment, reflecting ourselves off and out through the thick window. The height would always remind him of those suicide days.

I think I'll be going now.

Yes. They turned from the light.

What are you working on at the moment? I asked,

solemnly.

An underground samizdat, something for the shits, the lords and the mongrels.

We laughed. Simple then.

Take a look. The Old Man handed him a pamphlet.

The first line put him off: *SUCKLING FROM THE TEET OF GROUP DESPERATION.*

Think I'll leave it. Laying the paper down on the cut-up table.

Your choice. But Metro Polis is growing, I trust you've heard. And the O Press too. That's what the pamphlet's about. It's a warning. They're taking over news, taking over information. Complete propaganda, right down to the last word, said the Old Man.

I've seen it, but they've got some valid points from what I've read. He had to be deposed, he was a dictator, an evil man.

The Old Man shook his head and scoffed. Do you really believe that? Have you learnt nothing from our time, our talks together?

But they're right on a lot of issues, and it's efficiently written to boot. Sometimes you have to intervene. I was on deadline then. It was the humane thing to do.

Ugh, don't start with that efficiency lark. Efficiency has nothing to do with art. And humanity? Please. That's the direction of a subtle twist of truth. The hypocritical reversal of values. And if anything, good writing makes it worse. Makes it more convincing. Journalism used to be about ideology, before singular reforms and messages. But now they have none, and as soon as a crisis begins to loom they stop questioning anything and follow orders completely. Follow the line, the Old man said.

I was silent as I moved toward my exit. I looked at the old photographs on the walls. The world had aged so much since then, and the Old Man with it. There he was in all manner of places, all over the world: the dusts of the Middle East, the jungles of Southeast Asia, the riv-ers of South America, wearing that uniform. Carrying that smile. How he'd changed in those years, his skin and mind completely renewed, yet withering. For the worse, I thought.

You can take a bowl of soup if you like, the Old Man said, interrupting his train of thought.

I looked around at the fleas circling the stove.

Yeah, think I'll be off then. Keep it up old man, if you can, eh.

I can't. He said without smiling.

Chuckle.

You really are a bit of a chuckle brother aren't you? Go on, get out of here. He said, feigning offence, closing the door with a forgettable click.

The hallway was refreshing after the dank mess, but he seemed to always breathe a little easier sitting around that flat. The desk showed verve, showed life. Though his ideas spoke like paranoia, spoke like a blindness to him, and many would agree, there was a certain earnest belief behind them. An earnestness that showed what it meant. The Old Man had sacrificed a lot for his belief. Did that make him the fool?

He moved on down the corridor again. He would be tired, the eyelids dripping over his sockets, press the button for the lift.

Wait again. Dream again.

CHAPTER TWO

From the first day he had noticed movement in the rooms opposite, Samstag had begun a kind of recording in his mind. The walls were white, and along them ran empty bookshelves, perimeters of photographs on the walls, arbitrarily placed along even lines, up, down and diagonal, documenting those people's lives up until a point forgotten. From this angle he could only vaguely see what figures and landscapes the frames held.

In one, a small group of girls, teenagers, one leaning over another, a third standing arms outstretched at the back, celebrating some forgettable occasion. Captured in that pose and eternally joyful.

His eyes switched across from each picture to the next. A couple standing, in embrace, seemingly ignoring the camera, existing outside the moment captured, a white sky and a green meadow, a tree, an embrace, the image of love so consistently framed but amiss within the camera's grasp.

Samstag imagined walking through their flat, filling the rest of the room, the parts that, from his view, remained invisible. He laid a cabinet on the floor on the far wall, a soft and old sofa of modern design stretching from wall to door. He dropped a plant pot in the corner. A mirror on the wall.

He walked through the room in his mind, looking at the pictures, becoming the keen voyeur of their intention. He picked up small items of nostalgic sentimentality, handling them with his clean, soft digits. A pebble, a rock, a shell from a sandy coast. A ticket stub and a memory. Erasure of all else. The blinds that shielded his phantasy, the string that drew them up and down, he played with it in his mind. He tugged it in a loose grip and the click-clacking followed, the slats half way down now shooting upward at the ceiling.

On those first days the blinds were always up, they were unaware. He felt it no violation of their privacy to watch them and their existence, for their life was his life and they shared it all. For him, to exist was for them to hold existence too. There was no violation. There was no voyeur.

During those first evenings he watched. He noticed the bare room, always the television communicating some progression of relatable images. The secret man in there working for her pleasure. His bobbing head and shoulders lurched forward and back in the dim light of the tube. He had watched him giving her a massage many times. On most nights he would be offering some favour, some relief from the tease, after time spent sitting immovable on the sofa. Scenes flashing by.

She would walk teasingly into the room, through the doorway from the bedroom, past the door where coats, jackets and scarves hung delirious. The light in the bedroom shone, the plants and vase of flowers illuminated at the window. The chest of drawers below the mirror, the sheet reflecting out and revealing more frames, more trinkets.

She measured each step forward. A dream, an obsession, into the room. And I felt pity for him. He looked up at her and then back to the wall. An unresponsive log. She rested a leg down, his non-reaction fuelling her ambition, her body sliding through seduction next to him in his place. Her appetite growing. He imagined her hand dripping onto his neck and playfully massaging. Gentle. But he ignores it and focuses his gaze outward. She follows his line of vision and relaxes back too.

Poised on the wide cushions she stretches her legs, toes pointed at the ceiling, pretending not to notice his slight turn. Acute hips that turned her feet inward. He resolves to play the game and joins in, resting a hand on her thigh. Nothing is said. Innocently she lowers her head sideways onto his shoulder and they watch together.

Minutes and moments pass as he watches from his window. He keeps himself busy by shuffling two decks of cards together, the red diamond backs fluttering in between the blues, and they mix. He wonders how many times he would have to shuffle to get them back into their original order. How many times a clown blows a balloon. How many times a horse gets the whip.

He thinks it all impossible. Looking up and through the glass he wonders silently, counting, calculating the odds in his head. He returns his eyes to the life opposite.

CHAPTER THREE

The next day I went back to see the Old Man, having forgotten the sack in which I carried my wares.

Hello hello hello, fancy seeing you here again so quick. He said brightly.

Yeah, hi. I replied without humour, and strode in, noticing he had perked up a little, because of the chalks. But I wasn't feeling amicable, certainly not in the mood for our chats, or our games. I needed mine.

I forgot some stuff, I told him, walking forward to move him out of the way.

Oh. You did?

We went through, to the back again where the bag was last seen.

Right, where was it. We looked around the table and the chairs, papers fell as we searched under books and newspaper cut-outs, old towels and dishrags.

It's not here, I announced to him, accusingly.

Don't look at me. If you left it here, it must still be here. I haven't moved anything of yours.

How would you know? You're fucking off your face. I had turned on him.

All right, little buddy, calm it down. We'll get yours,

don't worry.

No, we won't you old bastard, where are they? I stared him down, then aligned my gaze toward the table, ripping sheets into the air, hunting, feverish. There's nothing out there, they haven't got shit. I screamed, losing the hold on control. Everyone's getting shut down you fucking old cretin, don't you realise? I did you a favour, now where's my shit?

Easy there, we'll get some, we'll get some. He repeated, trailing off as the white blobs in his sockets searched the room. Rolling up and down in his head, the eyeballs were always on. They never got a rest. Whether in sleep or in light, the eyes had no off switch. And closing the lids never helped.

We'll get some. We'll get some, he kept saying.

I left the chrome of the high rise. A man in black stood at the base, eyes darting around in his skull. We clocked each other as I came through the door.

Code. Search.

What?

Code. I'm going to need to search you.

There was nothing on him, just a pencil and paper. He was glad he had left it all upstairs.

Where've you been today, do you live here?

No, just visiting.

Who?

A friend.

Which flat?

What's it to you?

Code. Which flat?

What are you, an officer or a reporter?

Code, last time, what flat number?

Flat 1789.

There's no 1789. Code. I'm taking you in.

The man in black had produced a hood from his belt and covered the arrestee's head. He was neatly inserted into a safe seat in the back of the vehicle. He was familiar with the situation, it had happened to him before. But the vehicle was different. The seat had been hollowed out to the bottom of the automobile so that his posterior was at the base of the car, sat on thin sheet metal. There was no seat, as such, to speak of. It was a hole. There was no room for manoeuvre. He was strapped down in such a way that he could move only his hands and his feet. He felt it futile to resist such a forceful arrest, he just sat in the back and waited.

They pulled away with a jerk and sped to wherever it was he was being taken.

He was yanked from the hole by his head and shoulders. The sound of the vehicle's closing doors reverberated through his chest. He was nudged then pushed forward. The area was silent, no sound, not even the breeze.

This all seems a little inappropriate.

We'll see about that.

He heard the man in black talking to another as they entered the building.

Got another one, boys. He said bumptiously.

Good work, sir.

Right, right.

Name.

It was silent.

Name.

He got a jab.

Name.

He could hear the reporter step forward on the concrete floor with a heavy boot. All sound drowned out as he vomited in his hood and collapsed on the squeaking floor. How much does it cost to save a man?

His chasing loose laces kicked angrily but obediently behind, ripping the pavement up as his scurry grows more desperate and shuddered.

Following.

CHAPTER FOUR

I wasn't sure what they were planning. Plan D as they called it. They wouldn't let me in on it. It was a conspiracy.

This is my flat, I live here. You can't come in and take it over and not let me in on what you're doing. I have just as much a say in it as you do. If you're using me as bait or if you're using me as the setup, I simply won't stand for it. These quarters are mine. You must tell me.

But I didn't say anything, I let them get on with it, and ghosted by the door frame invisible.

Their voices: We have to get on the inside. I heard the Old Man say. Fight demon with demon. Make him become one.

It won't be as simple as that. That's plain naïve, won't work. There's no telling what he'll do.

It's only naïve if we don't take it as far as we can, take it all the way.

I know what you want, but I don't know if we can pull it off.

Come on this isn't some heist, there's no risk here.

Of course there's risk. There's always risk.

Risk of what?

Failing. And that would mean our freedom.

Don't get all melodramatic on me. That's all we had to give before. But now we have more. And it'll be worth it.

I stood at the precipice, the cliff swaying beneath me. The world and the external swirled inward on my thoughts and cut all dimensions to white. I poured the boiled water into the mugs. I was their butler. But I didn't mind. This would be strong material.

When I awoke it was dark. The hood and all my clothes had been removed, replaced with white overalls. I could see a steel door with a small, post box sized hole. The windows were a series of slits in the wall and allowed only the gentle beam of a security light. I was laid out on the floor next to a metal bed that had no mattress. A camera in the corner shone a single beam of light onto my forehead, splitting onto my eyes. I winced.

Yes?

Code. The camera spoke.

A rail on the other side of the door slid and clicked. The post box opened to reveal a pair of smiling eyes.

We know just who you are, Mister Sonntag.

Congratulations there, that must have been difficult. Read can you?

Very good. The eyes spoke without irony, without humour. Get up. They said.

Why?

Code (angrily). Get up or we'll make you get up. Or if you prefer, we'll make it so you never have to get up again (calming down, smug).

Yep. I'll have Number Two then.

The eyes creased, smiling again. Post box shut. Door open. The four reporters stormed in. I passed out.

One white bar. Two white bars, more. Then no picture, no lights, no hum. *Laughter, crying, baiting, resting. All tease. Silenced. The eyes are looking up. Around. Scuttling and useless. Minions and pawns among us. Hands reach. I hear the birds. They are not singing. The ground is cracked. Rumbled beneath like it was all caving in. Whimpers and shouts mixed across the white and black. Glasses shook 'til they exploded, fingernails shattering, eyeballs split, all of it thrown into some godless bonfire. I heard the hundreds of doors swinging and slamming, timid happiness seeping out. Modest silence followed for some time, whispers in the darkness. Inquisitive conspiring, some expected hypocrisy. Those sleeping in beds continue to serve; they are now deaf to shooting and silent murder. Their mouths are spent and hands withered. They call it virtue. I termed it war. My unblinking eye stared toward the mountain. Once there was a figure who moved upon it, across and sometimes upward. The harsh light gleamed into the room, I look away to the corner and it disappears away smaller and smaller. An animal moves raggedly down the mountain. Fast. Tumbling leaps. I am weeping. Many are the fallen. Quiet steady voices speak in far off places; human and domesticated. Using all of the flesh and the tissue, every cell held tight and cleverly resounding. The gloom had dropped. Hills and perception torn apart.*

A man shrinking, his porch around him. A wife, her hair barbed, as if it wore her. A small word, the turgid ear. The tiny feet, the swallowed street. A steady slew flowing down the mountain and all around them. Something had ended that so now we have to circle the remains. A quivering breath.

This is getting a little tedious. The voice spoke again.

I agree.

The eyes reappeared.

The mechanisms on the door unlocked and it opened.

Hello.

They slid me out on my back. I stared upward. Placid. I could see a hallway over-lit and housing many more doors and rooms I assumed to be just like my own humble quarters. They slipped on the same old hood. Black. It reeked of sweet vomit.

Code. Stand him up.

Yessir.

Right, Sonntag. Welcome. I'm sure you've heard of us now, haven't you? Don't bother answering, anything you say will only hurt your position further.

I stood there.

The room was dressed like a makeshift interrogation room, just with an added executioner high up in his chair, behind a desk built to eye level. He looked down on me, leaning out of his domain. He had a face like a leather mask. Eyebrows that bore a dreary weight. His flesh all rounded and loose at the cheeks, the jaw too, jowls dangling as he spoke.

Code. He said. Tell us. What is it that you do for a living, Mr Sonntag?

I. I try.

And what does that mean, exactly?

I try to... get it out. The living.

The judge frowned. Be more specific, no more of this floweriness. He said. What is it you've you been up to?

I was visiting a friend.

Who is your friend? We know who he is, but what is he to you?

He's my teacher. He taught me to think.

What did he teach you to think?

I don't know. The things that I think, he must have taught me.

You take no responsibility for your own thoughts? Were they planted there by your friend alone?

No. Well. No. They are mine too. I can agree or disagree. That is a choice. My strength.

So what is it that you're thinking?

What do you mean?

Come now. You know what I mean. What is that you think goes on here?

In this place?

Yes, this place.

Torture. From what I see.

Torture of what? Of you?

Yes, torture of me, of my living. I began to feel weak, like the life was leaking out of me through the skin.

Amusing. Have we no right to torture you as you torture others?

I do not torture others. I quivered out the words, struggling with pronunciation.

Come, what is it that you do with your days? You scribble on notepads, notepads we have here, with us, would you like me to read?

No. Don't. I do not torture others in the way you've tortured me. You've beaten me, with your hands and your tools. You've tortured my mind.

Have we? But we have only taken you here for questioning, your own resistance has been your torture.

I didn't ask for you to come and take me in. I said. My

voice quivered. I shook from within.

Didn't you now? All must be accounted for, Mr Sonntag. And here, your writing, this, have others asked you to judge them?

I do not judge them. I only observe. It's just for myself. My own eyes.

Your eyes are the fountains, from which you create. In which you see what you must see. You spend your days going here and there, taking what you will and giving nothing. Spluttering nonsense.

Pause.

I have not judged.

"*The Worms protrude from the apple*." Did you not write this? Or are you simply a popinjay?

I... My hand did, yes.

Oh, then it is your hand that judges. Bring it here.

I raised my hand.

Here. The judge ushered him closer. Lay it there. Pointing at his high bench. Let me see the hands that think for you.

Here. Putting my hand down.

Then this is the hand that judges. Look at my hand. Are they not the same?

No, they are not. They are very different.

I disagree. To do so is my strength. And behind it is held reason. I have virtue. I see your hand there, made of its bones and its flesh, I see the nails yellowed and smooth. Look here at my hand. They are the same.

I looked at the hands hanging over the bench.

Bring in the other. The judge said finally, his head directed at the door.

From the back of the room the door creaked open. A man entered, he had on the same white overalls, and staggered toward the bench. Forced by uniforms from the sides.

Here, meet Sams.

His face was sullen, deadened around the eyes and mouth. He moved with a lurch.

We looked at each other, he with a timid stare from under his brow. I looked back to the bench.

Look at his hands. The judge demanded. Look at them.

Sams raised his hand. The bones had been smashed under the skin, yet it still dangled there from his wrist.

I looked into Sams' face, which had turned away to the far walls. He stared out the window into the courtyard where through oily glass the birds played. A blue one, a red one, and a white pigeon with brown-tipped feathers. He stared in the silence.

Do you know what happened to his hand? Do you know what he did with his hands?

I stuttered an answer, having the feeling that my hand too could look the same with the wrong response. Yes. I said.

We shattered it. The boy cannot follow Code. Had a sudden change of heart. He said his hands had done things, like you, and that he'd been taught them. But he stood there and took it. Old Sams here is in the minority. He thinks himself a Knight, don't you Sams? A Great One.

Sams stood there limp in his skin, his head tilted to the side, watching the birds. They hopped, wings fluttering, beaks pecking at the earth.

He doesn't speak much now. Do you Sams? The judge taunted him. Sams remained blank.

He wobbled on his feet but continued staring.

The judge peered at me and I looked back before breaking eye contact with another check on Sams.

We shatter it anew every once in a while. Would you like to watch perhaps? He's due for another one quite soon.

Sams winced but remained in control, holding his stare.

Do I have a choice? I asked.

That is a good question. But yes, of course you do, Mr Sonntag. You have a great choice ahead of you. You can watch. Or you can stop us. If you wish to try. But think about it, think with your hand. Look at yours and look at his, they are not the same, are they? But they can be. We will give you time to choose, so do it wisely and with your heart. For that is what we want, hearts. Not minds.

You write, you struggle. You try to create. But what is it that you really want? I think we can offer it to you. We know we can offer it to you. We have made it happen for thousands before you. Recognition is what you crave. Recognition of your work, your endeavours. And it's a great and noble struggle you put yourself through, yes. Noble, but misplaced. This we can help with. This we can solve. Work for us, write for us. But write with direction. With purpose. With a message.

I waited, not knowing my own fate, but knowing my answer. I went rigid, as a fly before a spider.

The judge spoke again: Take him away... Goodbye Sams, see you soon, my boy.

I watched Sams traipse to the rear where the guard, sneering with the wide split of his mouth, opened the door and followed him out.

What now?

You tell us, Mr Sonntag. You have a choice; we have laid it before you. You have heard of Metropolis, yes?

Yes, but not much.

You have seen Metropolis?

I nodded.

Then you know. I do not have to explain. But realise this, there are others who have given me different answers, others who were stronger than you. They are no longer with us. They thought with their heads. And that was where they received their judgment.

I nodded.

You choose.

I spent the night staring at the walls, thinking of Sams. The bricks stared back at me, uniform and bleak. What was I but a brick? The mass before me split and became singular, I saw each one segregated, the gray cement shaping the perimeter of each one. Did I want to be a brick, or the cement, or the wall? I sighed heavily. I looked down at my feet.

Even my thoughts were becoming trite.

What good could come of my writing, really? I looked to the door, the isolation that had an answer. Jeers drifted through the building into my ears. I imagined Sams' screaming face as they hammered down on the jelly of his hand, over and over. It was cowardice I felt. I was unworthy. But there would always be a Judge, and always a Sams.

And always a Sonntag.

This did not comfort me.

I couldn't stand up to anything, not them, not even my own mind.

I thought of the Old Man and where he must be. Perhaps that's what the judge meant when he spoke of the others stronger than me, unbreakable.

The words began to drain into my thoughts. I felt weak and useless.

I stared at my hands as I began to fall asleep.

The recurring nightmares. I observe from a distance. But I feel up close.

I sit atop the galloping hooves of gigantic horses. They thunder the way beneath them in earthy deafening thuds. The surge is uncontrollable. But it is not a race.

It is some medieval scene, the horses are dressed, masks cover their faces. Their speeding bodies throw me up and down, I cannot remain where I sit. I fall down, miles and miles, through the desert black and land running, amongst the stomping hooves.

I try hard to avoid them.

I succeed for a time and I say: I don't want to play.

But it is not up to me. It is up to them to stop.

I can see their black eyes.

The breath that runs out in the slipstream.

I continue to run.

The earth is cut up all around me.

I can see the way out over the horizon, but it is indistinct, melting.

And I cannot make it.

I wake up with the feeling that the room has disappeared out to nothing.

Around me is dark space.

But I am awake.

I am cold and weak.

CHAPTER FIVE

Training began the next day.

We sat in front of machines, screens blinking at us as we typed into them. The keyboards sung with the hitting of keys. Typing the same words over and over, copied from sheets handed to us at the start of the day, stuffed into the packed post box.

Two rows of us sat at gray desks, lined up in that small room. Plain, empty desks made of solid colour and clean surface. White overalls and machines mixed in, like a factory, but white and satisfying, very much unlike a factory. A guard patrolled us as we typed, a scene that recalled the day I came off medication. He was the only security they had there, but still none of us put up any resistance.

I thought back to the Old Man and how I could easily have thrown him out of the building that day. When the memories came back they reassembled again into hatred. For some reason I refused to take responsibility and I began to shape him out as the reason for all my problems before I'd joined Metropolis. It seemed sensible. He had held me down and tried to control me. Those stupid, pointless games we played. And all that vomit that he taught me about expression and about truth. It all seemed to melt away now. The Old Man only existed in bad memories, painful images in my mind, of suffocation and fear. An object of disgust.

My mind sailing back to the days of my childhood. But the memory was without context, merely an island in the stream of my consciousness. I pictured Grandpa there, trousers rolled up to his knee, standing in the water – urging me to come out. The sun dripped over the horizon and the water shone back. The thoughts were all backward.

His big arms and his teeth called me closer, and I stepped through the sandy beach deeper into the water. Clouds and laughter formed, sunlight beckoned. The image switched, all the colours wiped across. My head swings low over the lapping shore, held in the air by the leg, past the water as it flashes by, my face skims it, around and around, as my head dips in and the wet punch smacks my jaw, and the side of the face, I inhale, sucking in air from the plain sky. I'm plunged in again, pure fear and suffocation is all I feel. He doesn't stop, the memory drips over my eyes. The Old Man keeps swinging the child over the water as fluid enters the lungs, and I feel as if the world is drowning with me.

BLACK

IRIS OUT

I return to the room. Turning my head around, struck by the concentration and sincerity bleeding across all the faces. There was this feeling that we were learning something there, like we'd been taught a protected but sordid secret that we all wanted in on, and we weren't going to tell.

Everything else that used to matter slid away like golden butter in the sun. Many of the mouths smirked, the eyes still unresponsive, mumbling as we repeated the same words over and over. Through our fingers, through our lips. But we enjoyed our refreshed purpose with baneful vigour.

Out there it was grim, there was no work, no hope. Horror and disgust. We were reminded of that daily. In there we were given security and virtue. We could breathe a little easier.

Life, Work, was a joy. And it burned incandescent on the black wick of our fanaticism.

I lie on plain beds empty as my thoughts, my words, wandering and a little worried about the other sleeping heads. The blue inks are twinkling shut as I watch the glitter descend the wall, leaving a shimmer on the ceiling. And Nothing. This is some false awakening.

I am lost. Like the form of the spinning track, laid

on plastic dancefloors: swirling lights and dropped hats. This hollow just doesn't feel real. Or right. Looking into required eyes I sometimes tilt, but the sighs and darting eyes lose all and any ground covered. Long sighs pulling my hair out over emotions waving goodbye.

I do crying expressions I cannot shake for anyone. But I know anything I get back will just as soon be going anyway. I am under a window with a head on a silver trophy – a thing carved with no attention. Only bitterness.

I am as regretful and replaceable as the hanging side mirror of some rusted automobile, but harder to find. Some heads are opened, some aren't – echoing laughter that fills unwanted hallways and phone booths standing anonymously.

I am down and out, there is no railroad out of here: no ticket to buy to make the journey any smoother. I don't want easy, or any of that.

Difficult is what some people like, but what's wrong with lazy. Is it collected family egos and eyes weighing down, or another inner circle that can ignore perdition and this active limbo?

Perjury of a life before or after, I do not know. I look at the tips of my digits and down the bone surrounded by soft flesh to the palm. Veins green in my wrist. A terse forearm reaching for my abdomen. Shallow, I look under beds of hate. I can sleep there, with all the other broken and contented swine pieces.

I don't need, want or stand for wallowing anecdotes dressed with towelled necks, vomiting throats or open chords. Don't tell me.

I can't give you any more or any else. I just can't. It will be over soon.

Cuff me and take it all away so I can do no wrong again. Rhyme for me – kick my teeth as you set them on stone. Push me up against the wall and empty your hand into mine. I want an end but can't have it. It is just numb fragments that I want to put my head to. Because I need. Need. Cry for it all day and all night appearing unassuming, but there is some faulted plan in this, that I know will win out only if I let it. I cannot be saved.

I'll walk through the alleys and dim streets 'til I set my eyes on it and my heart. To shake hands with it and read your face. But it evades me, again and hopelessly again. Organs straining in my toy abdomen. Leave me out in the cold where I'll belong. Nestled under snapped shards I can sleep with. Art of darkness on heart of light that might feed me something true and worthy. Don't watch the visions, sell them. I just stare and they flow past my hair. I. I. Nothing can be pathetic until your churches, houses, temples, rooms and synagogues have built over you. Growling like death snaps in the morning.

Crawling and needing is the knife that slides in. Separating mine from fiction. Hang your scarf and stay a while. Through a night with your water thighs against mine and me lost in you. I don't want to be found when that happens. It will all stream like a hot spring. Unfocussed lights will not matter, when I am blind your heart will still beat in my vision and you will hold my infinity in your closed palm. Played until I cease. Anyway, all I have are broken bones. Flat stones for skipping across oceans to brotherhood.

Drowning fear keeps the masses from really falling, and so when they are made to take a long step off tall stairs there is panic and confusion. Things like that have always been, and exist in us all. I am told to sell. Some to the awake, some in coma. Even so, it is that snake which pushes us down into our own stomachs, down into filth. Asleep to what is possible, only sat in one direction and not embraced by warm arms of interest, or even understanding.

Neon tubes filled with futile, absurd wants. Set on edges of welfare we will all fall deep. But it will be more than giving up. I have not known purity for any of my moments. Sentimental alleviations and sympathies out of pouring wine jugs. Complex marionettes dried in karma and destiny. If you believe in that sort of thing: Play the strings to the march of brass and gold. And watch it all shine under water.

Do the crackheads and the junkies still have more in common with me than these silent suited armies? I do not know. Opened minds to realities of shadows and what *sleeps in gutters and under bridges. Under ground. And earth.*

Sleep in arms this night and see. Play a hymn for this hundredth requiem. A last note for the big bad word.

Soft eyes and transparent windows to beliefs clay-set but gratefully flaking.

I need rest from these artificial glows and false auras. Set me apart and treat me so. Leave me if I do not respond.

You and none of us are unique. Just some regurgitation of some Dadaist god, and an unoriginal one, whose naturally homogenised laws will play out all these words on a string.

Your soft lips as giving to my rhythms as your intense expression as you leave me.

Warm and shattering of my innards. That look. Flies me away from this communicated irritation, and I will soon let go.

Villains of innocence watch whilst the room is heated from below. Avoiding the envious cold that snatches a now-detached feeling of pity.

Civil allegiances to forgotten values. Pedantic displays of memory and study. Show us what you think you know and recite us the rest. Stop strangling me with your glances.

A strain of free wing closed over nesting hard-boiled eggs. Errors of time and terror.

Sleep now and ebb to alternate worlds.

Talk to me, tell me what you've seen whilst I rest from this 'hour' and the next. Strangled breaths from the cage you have sought for many of your perceived years. You cannot tell me anything new. Make me more uncomfortable than I felt possible. Insult the room and yourself, then laugh alone.

My ghost will crack the shell and it will despair whilst screaming, HASN'T THE OUTSIDE TURNED ITSELF IN? At least some release.

The trampling demon horse above me, some wandering lost soul chased.

I'm back. I want to play.

Loud, dumb revelations like: Life is just a ride. Rewind that one, don't repeat. Religion? Not for your reasons. A mouth moving, pointless and pedantic, all worldly judged consequence. Like forcing marshmallows through keyholes.

What do they want?

What comes out the other side can never compare to original form. Can it?

But wait for the evolution, then decide. And know your decision has or will be changed. In its loathing and drunken reflection we seek skies black that will calm with their slow anonymous twinkles. I can only look up and stare, gormless, at mirages and paintings of what may be there. I will gladly close my eyes to it, then vomit quietly.

It is hard to pinpoint sleep, its dull candour. I will be awake for as long as you can bear. Eyes aching. Too repetitive and I hope meaning something when read back.

The digital timers click past hours wallowing in remorse and egotism.

I am guilty of neglecting time and notes and royal coins dead as words in my pockets.

I can only dry what was once wet and alive, panting like some far off jaguar or swollen horse – ridden and abused for markets of gain and profit. Numbers dead, too. Words dead, still. All the rest is living, breathing?

Urged on by rising suns and setting moons on tides that escape hands plastered by salt and sand, clutching is a losing battle.

Release is what the god of wine will urge on unfinished scrolls, recording wild hedonism sleeping under despondent duvets. Tie down the blanket and strangulate.

I will not wake up.

CHAPTER SIX

There is a constant and infinite realisation of this over and over and over: What it means to be in such a position. Trapped. All of us. Unable to break free for reasons created by outsiders.

But it seems a sentiment lost forgotten erased only for some to begin the Clutching. Horrific tones that deny, and viscous inks that resist, sliding down the opaque glass of reason thundered by rain and a compulsive need for escape.

A tree cut in the urban forest. Not everything on these hills and climbing mountains desires to be taught, automatic, leaning toward these machines swallowed in dust.

The sands and winds have time for neither and will become as hollowed and dead as the marionettes strung by all of the above. As dead as these words. These symbols. These flapping doors of connotation, definition and malleable meaning, left barely on their hinges. Melodramatic orchestrations do not slice the chords of cynicism, of truth, of the back-stages of this Theatre. 'Enlightened' intellect with fingers crawling as spiders' legs over the minds of some committee, some idea of their reconciled desires as emaciated as the hands that could have very well destroyed them, after creating them.

The days designed, what you do and what they are made of.

A blanket of mist penetrated by one eye all seeing all knowing – no feeling. Amongst invisible vines the confidence handed to them (those few) convinces the carnival and the farce of the city (spitting) hum (drum), intoxicated in taverns and cathedrals and stadia and living rooms – a violent requiem for the dripping mirrors that walk among us, occasionally saying 'Hello'. A fantastic nonfiction in flesh. The barbarians are no myth to opened eyelids and there is no reflection in their matte black pupils. There are more frightening images than running shadows from trees and walking walls.

So in your belief of etiquette and customs generated by archaic tradition, I am that choking indifference.

I thought back to the concrete room where the flower of this day had grown from. Or was it a weed. If I hadn't been so attached to that Old Man, to thinking that he had something to tell me, something to teach me, then I may still be out on the street. No, that wasn't true. There was no If. No Why. I cast my notes into the steel bin. I had gotten it all out now. The final bile.

My breathing and my blood flowed along the river into the ocean beyond ours. There was only one way it could move. The striving and the struggle meant nothing.

We were picked up and carried without us knowing any different.

To begin somewhere. Yes. Training.

To begin with, there was no inherent meaning to the language.

Where there were supposed to be numbers or names there were blanks we left space for, to be filled in later. The rest seemed like perverted cliché, hyperbole and exaggeration. Building illusions of supposed truth, of enlightening reality, when all was dark, electricity removed.

There were a few varieties of template, we would work one for an hour then switch, then back to the first one, and so on. We would alternate all day. The white pages kept coming. Over a week we covered about ten different formulae, learning them by heart until we typed them without the post box morning sheets.

Our rooms had become homes, our prison became security. No one struggled with the work, it was quite mindless, and in fact we all thought a machine could have done it. But they wanted us to do it. *We* wanted to do it. And they required a human face for the machine. So at the end of every article we would have to sign our names, followed by Code.

At first we protested, our work slow and ponderous, our typing laboured, eyes leaving screens. We wanted back our glorious freedom of expression, but we soon learnt. It was for the better. The formulae spoke for us, and spoke through us. It delivered everything concisely and included all of the information the readers required.

Tell the story, direct, get the quotes, get the angle, if you haven't got an angle then work one, slot the events into a narrative, then leave the last line for balance, if there is space. If there is time.

Keep it short, concise. That's what they want. Beware complications. Leave out complexity. There's no space for it. No time for it.

We burned off the fat. Of our verbose and effusive writing, narrowed our thoughts and removed all doubt. Our history of miscommunication forgotten. Here we unlearnt all of the unnecessary habits we had indoctrinated ourselves in, and now we delivered words along a line, a direct communication of meaning from one to another. Gone was the frustration. Gone was the feeling that everything I wrote had been said before, during my foolish years. As long as the meanings of the words never changed, I would be a grand communicator. But I worried that the meanings were shifting too much already.

Still, I felt rewarded by the Corporation, I was one of them and truthfully, that was all I had ever wanted. Days of trembling behind the page and the pen, waiting for validation, had been worth it. Now I had paid my dues. I welcomed the rewards with open arms. And I cursed wickedly the days I had lost at the hands of that Old Man.

Over and over we signed our names and began new templates, slightly altered each time but consistent in their meaninglessness. It felt familiar. Interchangeable events made to appear crucial to the Reader. The anyone.

We repeated a detached but lofty voice, I was beginning to dissolve into it. Written with esoteric knowledge hidden from the masses, but *of* the masses *for* the masses. Our works were desolate of any 'information' in its truest sense. Mechanical, like digital sex. It was data without context, and told the people nothing. We were self-regulated and out of control. The things we wrote were like raindrops in the sun. And we didn't expect anyone to know any different, or to Think.

We heaved over news articles on a handful of subjects. They revolved around crime, business, shootings, bombings, stabbings and State Visits. The rest swept across Entertainments, celebrity, names. The television listings on the same unchanging page. Full sheets of large colour photography that our budget slid into, and away, and back in a cycle. A cycle of commercial media, without a voice for the bottom two-thirds of the broken ladder. But we hung on to the top rungs.

Hidden images behind the amplified speaker of modern news. We'll never touch the lives of these people, instead we'll divert. With trivia of varying degrees, and gossip. Or the latest diatribe in the wars of perception. And get paid.

Then there were foreign policy updates. Someone was supposed to have been visiting somewhere ███████ to promote ██████████: ████████ visited ████████ ██ today on an unexpected state visit to boost support for growing ████████████.

███████████ arrived in ██████████████ today, pushing forward the ██████████, which has seen staunch opposition by militant supporters of ████████ in the ██████████ region.

██████████ cruised over the city of ████████ targeting ████████████ with laser-guided ████████, closing in on the ██████████ insurgency lead by what some term the militant ████████████ group.

██████████ insurgents reportedly killed ██████ civilians, in new statistics drawn up by the ██████ department of the ████████. ████████████████ ████████ disputes the ████████████████████ ████████████████.

██████████ coalition forces were alleged to have targeted a base for ████████████ insurgents earlier this morning. ████████████ were injured in the raid.

The international community has condemned last

week's attacks by ███████ in the ███████ region of ███████████████.

A victory for the growing campaign against human rights violations in ███████ today, as democracy forges itself in ███████. The people of ███████ rejoiced in the streets, waving flags and banners, announcing 'Welcome, ███████' and 'Thank you, President ███████.'

███████ state TV has aired what it says is a confession by a ███████ soldier under threat of execution for ███████.

In the interview shown on ███████, ███████ purportedly admits conspiring to assassinate ███████ and indiscriminately targeting ███████ civilians.

Thousands queued over night to get their hands on the latest ███████ from ███████████████, released in the early hours this morning. The release of the new ███████ saw fans gathered outside the ███████ ███████ headquarters for a view of the next generation ███████, which offers new ███████, updated ███████████████) and improved ███████.

A ███████ teenager has been shot dead close to ███████'s border, ███████ says, as at least five other ███████ were wounded elsewhere.

███████ was killed in ███████ by ███████ ███████ fire near ███████ the ███-

run ████████ said.

The ████████ peacekeeping force said it was not aware of any ████████, but military sources said warning ████████ had been ████████ in the area.

A shocking ████████ struck the ████████ today as ████████ extremists targeted ████████ headquarters.

A ████████ cruiser was attacked and sunk today. The ████████ deny any involvement but the ████████ Prime Minister condemned ████████ for what the ████████ community are calling a "blatant act of aggression."

████████ Generals are reporting a troop surge today in retaliation to the ████████ ████████, following their attempt to take hold of the ████████ province. Security forces have now secured the militant ████████ stronghold.

A spike in violence in ████████ today as ████ ████████ targeted ████████, seeing at least ████ ████████ personnel killed in what ████████ officials are calling an "unwarranted attack" and "a clear act of war".

████████ merged with ████████ today as progress was made in the reform of the new ████████ ████████ as ████████ called for new sanctions against the ████████ regime.

The number of civilians killed or injured in ███████ ██████████ has rocketed to ██ per cent, despite a fall in the number of casualties caused by ████████████████ forces.

More than ████ civilians were killed in ███████ ██████████ with another ████ civilians injured, the latest ████████████████████████ report showed.

The ███████████ and other paramilitary forces were responsible for ██ per cent of the casualties, jumping from ███ per cent last year.

A spokesman for the ████████████████ rejected the official ████████████████████████ estimate.

The ████████████████████ figures for civilian casualties were the worst in █████ years of conflict.

The radical ████████████████ group alleges the ████ ████████████████████████ settlements are ████████ ████████████████.

More casualties and ███ deaths today as ███████ ██████████ agitators surrounded the ████████████ embassy in what officials said was "an unnecessarily violent protest". A spokesman for the █████ administration said ██ ██ ██ ██, adding that ████████████ was the reason for tension in the region: "There is still hope for the peace process. It all depends on the ████████████ group's willingness to negotiate."

    Peacekeeping ▮▮▮▮▮▮▮ *suffered yet more casualties today as* ▮▮▮▮▮▮▮▮▮ *attacks struck in* ▮▮▮▮▮▮▮.

    ▮▮▮▮▮▮▮▮▮ *officials announced today that all combat troops will be withdrawn from* ▮▮▮▮ *as early as* ▮▮▮▮▮.

    The ▮▮▮▮▮ *administration is yet to comment on the figure for non-combat troops remaining as a security force during the hand-over period.*

    We went over and over until ▮▮▮▮▮▮ *had done everything possible in the* ▮▮▮▮▮▮▮ *to prevent the* ▮▮▮▮▮▮▮ *from stopping the* ▮▮▮▮▮▮ ▮▮▮▮ *process.*

Data without context. Normalise violence. Normalise horror. All about perspective. The correct perspective.

Officers, here begins your real training. Those first ones were easy. We want you to knuckle down now, grind out the real data. We want officers able to pick the right facts, pick the right quotes, go to the right sources, ask the right questions. And we need it fast and consistent. Carriages on the track, all connected, all toward the same destination. Let's go.

That was the second week. A quick week. Filtering out the unready, unprepared of us. We were energised from the practice. The unwilling were left behind. We congratulated ourselves as we punched out sentences and lines and stories in the new language. Anyone not wanting to jump on the rope was left hanging.

Gradually, we all began picking the same quotes, the right quotes. Intuitive almost. Untaught. But none of us seemed to notice anything strange about that. In fact we were rewarded. We were encouraged to build up weak narratives, fitting events into other events as if somehow related, as if somehow one led directly to the other. Order out of the chaos. No mystery to life, no pondering. Un-scientific streams.

We were encouraged to put events side-by-side in a teleological path that put things down to cause and reaction. Bees in the wind. Anyone coming away from the line was put back with some gentle words from a mentor. Some *friendly* suggestions. We were promised the chance for reward and prestige. We idolised and hoped we too would become the idols. We'd be fools to step out now. The brink of success awaited, only a door away. We'd come too far to squander our rights now.

The following week the templates became more intricate, more developed in their description of the ███████ ████████. But ultimately they all portrayed the same simplistic image, over and over. Legitimacy on one side, cruel ███████████ on the other.

With every word of the new language, renewed hope trickled down our eyelids.

At the end of the day, after eight hours of knocking at the keys, we went back to our canteen and sat, awaiting our meals, bunched up next to each other, even though that didn't seem necessary as we all just sat there re-imagining the templates when we weren't at our machines, consciously or not. Blank, blank, blank, went our minds. Our lips forming the 'B', as we thought-wrote it out in the air.

I ate, shovelling the fuel into my mouth, my fingers quivering as they held the spoon. They continued typing on invisible keyboards, knocking away absentmindedly at the machine that wasn't there. Blank blank blank, tap tap tap. We worshipped the new language they had given us.

We automatically discussed the meal afterwards, at the end of our break. Heads up from the kowtow.

But today: Would you care for a cigarette, Sonntag?

Yes, thank you, officer. I'd be delighted.

Stearns lit my cigarette. He was a senior editor, but he was kept in data to show us the ropes. He usually just let us get on with it. We took to the work quickly and after a fortnight, without question. He also smoked my brand of cigarette, which gave me some sense of dubious privilege.

Good meal today. Real, traditional grub.

Yes. Very hearty indeed. We pulled deep on our ciga-rettes, letting the smoke whisper out as we spoke.

You don't get that everywhere.

You certainly don't. Agreement was key.

Too much obsession with fancy, haute cuisine out there. Stearns said, plainly. His voice taking on the deep tone of some learned professor.

I agree.

Can't go to a restaurant and get real, traditional grub anymore. He swept his hand through his thick, red hair.

You certainly can't.

I like you, Sonntag. I think you'll go far. He said with-out really looking at me.

Thank you, sir.

D'you know why I think you'll go far? Stearns turned, all his features directed straight into me. The creased face of middle age, the freckles and the smug estate agent expression.

No, sir, why is it?

Well, for starters, you don't ask questions. Well, let me rephrase that. You only ask the *right* questions.

Yessir.

And secondly, you've got a keen memory for the templates. I've been watching your work. Very nice. I was like you. Eager. Just keep at it and you could be in my position not long from now.

Yessir. I became aware of my subservient responses but didn't want to break Stearns' generous mood. He had a way of ignoring us in the data room, often he sat at the head, face down tapping away, writing up new ones. But today he seemed glad to be here. Stearns looked around at the others smoking in the rooftop garden. Leaning in, he confided quietly.

They'll never get it, because they're slow and can't take orders. Code isn't the same to them as it is for you and me.

I nodded, glad in my heart that he had decided it appropriate to tell me of his pleasure working alongside me.

Thank you, sir.

He leant back. No, that's not flattery, Sonntag. It's the truth. You have no one else to thank but yourself.

And Metropolis. For the opportunity, I thought, but held back, not wanting to sound too fanatical or sycophantic. I'm very grateful for the compliment, sir, I said finally.

Now let's finish up our cigarettes and head home. My wife is waiting for me downstairs. Works in Human Resources down there. Taking her out for dinner and a show. A smile. A show of teeth.

Very good, sir. I replied, not quite knowing how to reply to his casual conversation. We put our cigarettes out in the tray that sat on the tall silver stand. I let him go back inside. Goodnight, sir. I said, as his reflection disappeared into the closing door.

You too, Sonntag. You too. He said morosely.

I stood atop the roof, putting off having to go back to the toilet. I lit another cigarette and watched the other interns. I would show Stearns what we were capable of.

There was a rebellion growing here. We would overturn the monsters, for to overcome them first you must become one.

Life continued for me most vividly within dreams. Work had overtaken my waking moments, but sleep had strongly reclaimed the ideas of my previous life. I kept it a secret from my superiors and the others, not wanting them to think me some romantic, falsely poetic wretch. My waking conscience accepted the freedom. Yet the night and its subconscious were different. I laid back deep onto the steel grate that was bed, and I slept.

Deep into black, I dreamt.

Here. Here is …

Here is the hall,

Here is the aorta, walking through the building and gliding over the paving outside. The row of chairs and dogs, the breaking glass and subsequent screams. Here is hell in a nightmare. White sheets above the pitch black, and falling. Here are the unfinished spirits. Here is the heart poured down drains, full bottles and ghouls – ghosts in glass, emptied or smashed. Here is the world, here are the poems here, the brushes of paint. Here are the songs, the sung, the yet to be, the lung. Here is an eye, a lip, a new way to embrace. Here is the water breaking on the beach. Here are parasols shielding the sun's fighting rays. Here are the days and coming morning. Here is the bed we share the coffee you make the food you prepared. Here are the clothes and the changing fashions. Here is consistency. Here is the way a man is taught to live. Here is the broken pencil. Here is distance growing with age. Here is pretending. Here is power and the way it lays, where it lies and how it thinks. Here is faith. Here is penetrating. Here is the population, expanding and dying. Here are apologies and bathtubs, falling water hot and made for steam. Here is liquid, here are the lakes, rivers the seas and the ocean and the journeys they make inland. Here is ferocity. Here are the stoics. Here is Empire. Here is the darkness. Here is the light, the sun and how one day it will all shatter. Here is the beginning. Here is the middle. Again, Here is the beginning. There is no end. You wrote the end. Here are cold stoves sitting crisp in the night and firing the days. Here are the ways we sat the ways we lay the ways we lie. Here is disaster - crackling treetops of jungle and dying hopes, breathing faiths. Here is time and the way it speaks and the way it could speak only one truth. Here are the spaces we filled and the way it all fell. Here is vision. Here is sight and warm reflection in your eyes. The way you moved. Here are the sighing waves, foam and salt. Here's to forgetting. Here is the burnt petrol the refined oil. The waste and the use. What is the use. Here are the hills in valleys. Here are snowy peaks – crashing mountains, talking volcanoes. Here are deep pockets filled with short fingers. Here are the pinstripes and straightened glass, their false majesty. Here are the words and how you meant them. Here are the windows and the sills and the eyes that stared out. Here is the shade and here is the tree. The eyes staring in. Here is relief. Here is reward and coming plunder. Here is the warm breeze and easy slumber. Here, the walking feet and talking heads. Here is ego. Here is right and there is wrong and all we have made up in between. Here it is all alike. Here is possibility here is truth here are the roofs and ceilings the shacks the favelas the slums the mansions and palace we built over it all. Here is desire and riches inside. Here are the guns laid on and the chosen handshakes. Here is gold, where did it fly, here is choice, here is destiny here is wavering beauty in the wind. Here is the sand the glass the wood the table, here is the dust we will all leave upside. Here is to circling and turning. Here are your hands your wrists. Here is galloping anger. Here is thundering vanity and how it's sometimes called rain, sometimes called drizzle. Here are the chains we had, the jewels. Here is personality. Here are repeated actions. Repeated words. They still have them. Here's to lost expression and unrequited dreams – longing and wanting. Here is the repaired machinery. Here are the billboards, posters, advertising. Here is manipulation. Here is art, here is the condor. Here are all the things I have never seen. Here is more. Here are all the hours I will miss. Here are all those things we never see and never will see. Here is nothing. Here is the single grain of sand. Here is the printed and the unprinted word. Here are screens and screams and the dead eyes that molest them. Here is stumbling. Here is the nightmare, here are the curtains that stood between. Here are climbing walls. Here is ink. Here is the paper and here are the olives. Here is convenience, held in storage. Here is the ash. Here are the fast breaths, and the last one. Here are the black beds. Here, the white sheets. Here, the carnivals and ice. Here is the soil. Here is the imagination of many and the actions of few. Here is government and all the words. Here is (God). Here is restraint and here is anarchy. Here are the walls falling and the fields left open. Here are the herds, the wilde-beest. Here is the innocent spear dipped in blood; man caked in iron. Here's to the mud. Here is the dirt. Here is pristine appearance and shined shoes on crumbling toes, sharp feet. Here is fruit, its changing sweetness. Here is strolling grass, here are bored families. Here are the housewives. Here is all the food they eat. Here are all the things they think. Here are the bowls of rice, bowls of soup. Here are the ones who sleep in streets. Here is their lost hope. Here is hope as a lie. Here is the world as owing to one man, and one man owing to the world. Here is humanity and all it has forgotten. All it will not remember. Here are the rocks that surround us and the cliffs that tempt them. Here is temptation. Here is the abstract. Here is the sheet. Here is the concrete. Here are the streets, the gates the doorways. Here is dropped money and flagrant tips from vacant eyes. Here is the beggar, the pauper, the coins in his hands and the nails in his feet. Here are the dog's sad eyes. Here is sunscreen and rain. Here are dried swimming pools here are factories here is the smog and death inside. Here is the clock and all it wants. The slow burning it churns up inside and out. Here are the pages turning and books closing. Here is the opposite. Here are the smashed plates of unfinished meals. Here is tension climbing across a dining table. Here is the silent church, the stupefying tavern. Here are the louts and their desperate cries. Here are closed doors. Here, the dripping ideas. Here, the institution. Here is asylum. Here is escape and sometimes there is none. Here are stories and realism. Here is pure invention. Here are newspapers, the tabloids the broadsheets, all the associated press. Here are untruths and freedom on a key. Here is what it is to be free. Here is what it is to run scared. Here is delight and here are dashed cigarettes. Here are the things we keep and the joys we smile and often cry. Here is dead skin and the dirty necks we hold. Here is the cowboy, the cheat and the empty hat. Here are the hours and the days. Here, the moon moving silently. Here's to looking up. Here are running minds. Here are the heaps growing and moss from the undergrowth. Here are the caves. Here are the symbols they use. Here are unbroken horizons. Here are the swaying sails. Here are the souls without sleeves. Here is wonder and happiness. Here is the rest. Here is the stolen horse. Here is unkempt hair. Here is pillage. The rapine. Here is the sword and here is honour. Here is disgrace and the words I have written. Here are the silent hordes and even quieter voices, words, sentences they have strung. Here is the penal colony. Here is hanging. Here is drowning. Here are all the tunnels the clouds the changing opinions; fashion. Here is dusk and how you felt. Here are soft glows and switched off lights. Here is the colour of darkness. Here is yawning, humming. Here is the Rapture. Here is falling. Here is awaking, awakenings. Here is neon. Here are moonless nights. Here are debilitating boils and desperation. Here is stepping off the bus, people sitting behind. Smiles and sorry. Here are rocked heads. Here is somewhere else. Here is sadness and charity. Here is what It means. Here is Bakunin, Kropotkin.

Here is the final vanguard the last stand. Here is change here it is all the same. Here is revolution. Here is torn flesh and blood lust. Here is hatred. Here is the present, the now. Here is the journey. Here's returning. Here is the opening riff. Here is harmony, perfection. Here is Keynes and blind wisdom. Here is the sage. Here is the shaman and his place on this earth. Here is the balance and ideals of egalitarianism. Here are changing winds and eternal voids. Here is Maslow. Here is Laing. Here is Bernays. Here is Huxley. Acrid revelation. Here are the wondrous females, slinking movements and sheer passion that all make such sense in a flash. Here is contentment and resting on laurels. Here is self-certainty and self-righteousness. Here are Bukowski, Fante and soaring birds. Here is you. Here is film and rolls of it. Here is Christmas in Trafalgar Square. Here is warm embrace, bellicose clutching and short goodbyes. Here is never goodbye. Here is how they will destroy it all. Here are the options they have and the holes they live in. Here are the lost forests. Here is opium. Here is mistaken glamour. Here is the syringe and loosened arms. Here is the random gesture. Overwhelming smiles. Here's to wrapping around it all and killing it. Here are the graveyards and their shifts. Here are flanks and eager bombs. Here, none of it is worth saving, here's to letting it live. Here is strategy and its futility. Here is understanding and non-acceptance and refusal. Here are lines of blue and seas of a darker shade. Here is confusion and panic. Suspended principles and neglected justice. Here are the courts of law and the weak hammers inside. Here is the space between your toes and when I was wrong. Here are the bouts of strength and lingering weakness. Here's to better, for worse. Here is matrimony and monogamy. Here are the legislators. Here is dance and imposed movement, thought and action. Here is rhyme and meticulous workings. Here are reins, puppets, marionettes. Here is philosophy and meaning and the cracks in the pavement. Here is miscommunication, satellites and hands in hearts thumping. Here are fits and comfort. Here is self-improvement. Here is muscle. Here is controlled laughter and the shy warmth held back. Here are cold wet feet and meeting hops. The tips of fingers wrapped around claws. Here is inquisition and small talk, the filler we never touched. Here is meaning. Here is sometimes and some times. Here is what we gave and what we thought possible. Here are quietly crossed legs and things we thought we could take back. Here is peace and relative peace and nothing like peace. Here is the insult. Here are the wars we experience and the lands left to wilderness. Kneeling, watching dead graves. Here is existence and life from death and death from life. Here are the flies and their rules. Here is the coming day soon when I will be forgotten and names and numbers ride on breezes out to nothing. Here are the lines in the air and words unspoken, men un-hanged, un-quartered or alive. Here are jet engines and concentrating eyes. Here is the taxi. Here are ages and epochs, invented dates of birth. Here are famous last words and famous first words. Here are washed minds and cleansed bodies. Here is paradox. Here is how sometimes we are allowed and sometimes we are not. Here is improved vision and stabbed eyes. The colours we see through and lights we turn on. Here is Epilogue. Here is the last wave, the last poem, the final insight and the ultimate illusion. Here are perfectly spelt words and perfectly formed legs. Perfectly uttered words and perfectly translated feeling. Here are goals and objectives. Here is why. Here is the way it would be and the way it was. Here is sun falling into sea and rising once more. One more time. One last time. Here are constant reminders to injustice and streaming channels under flesh. It is easy to cry for them but their relief will be the same as the rest. Here is a welcome. Here are the dogs that have lived too long. Here is the crying night. Here is fidelity. Here is the pregnant sky. Here is holiday. Here are deep, controlled heaves in our chests. Here is the wild bison. Here are clenched walls and falling shards around it. Here are grim realities we build. Here is depression, imposed suffering. Here is the unhatched egg. Here are feathers floating through ether. Here are the mystics, the big answers and short questions. Here are the crusades. Here is wisdom in ignorance. Here is the sail tied to the mast. Here are the tipped hats and requiem. Here are the 24 hours. Here is a move. Here is a checkmate. Here is falling down stairs. Here are open doors, opening-hours, and reflex glares. Livid eyes, through the heart and resistant to soul. Here is the W. Here's to grafted steel and iron mined from mountains. Here's to collided great gray stars. Here's to the scolded coffin laid in live soil. Here's to the rot in chambers. Here is heaven. Here is moving to places in the valley of the mind. Here are the trees that have grown from seeds we stole and made our own. Here are the inexplicables. Here is the nihilist. Here is the signature and abused exclamation mark. Here are the needs and unholy meetings. Here, tall towers and hidden arches. Here, mis-created minds, species unevolved. Here is the all of everywhere. Here is the hall plastered with prison breath, turning and smashing rosewood doors. Here is poesy. Here is meaning taken form at the root and reality. Here is blankness. Here is chalk. Here is the state of mind. Here is offering nothing, but all of it. Here are the strays. Here are unpaid tabs. Fresh fillets of beef, sunken wine chalices. Here are prizes and reward. Here is arrogance, here is self-satisfaction and small pieces in room-sized jigsaws. Here are the spies. The repeater shotguns. Chopped hogs and morning eggs. Refused requests. Mood swings in epic shapes. Swinging arms flying in carnal anger, at air, at nothing. Here is he who invented the Dragon. Here is non-believing. Here is the way they form. Here is the photograph and unobtrusively written stories. On walls, half-full half-empty beer bottles insisted upon the beach-front. Here is sifting necessary and unnecessary words, here is one added and why it is so denied. Here is judgement of unnecessary, here it remains judgement. Here are honest gestures mistaken. Here are close calls in the world they are perceived. Here is salt in the wound. Here are answered doors and ones left alone. Waiting. Lighting a cigarette and riding the bus. Here is style, and grandeur. Here is mundane opportunity, movement etched by severity. Here is the mud. Here is throwing heavy vomit. Here are peers. Here are planned journeys and expectancy, of what has been done, its reasons and insignificance standing tall on pages. Here is if feeling and emotion exist. Here is wet flow, littered fumes of ash in bottles. Here is sheer masquerade. Here are winners in competition. Here are arm wrestlers, playground fighters. Here is the noise. Here is the silence. Here is black mutilated laughter.

When I woke each morning I kept my eyelids held shut. Edging toward the darkness for more, I tightened my lids pushing back the eyeballs. I searched for the dark in there. I searched for my stigmata. I hunted the complete and pitch black night, but found only colours and light, shapes and shadows formed and blurry, but the optic silence never showing.

Could it be possible for man to invent some kind of drug that allowed every man and woman and child to experience lucid dreams, conscious dreams that meant all we wanted to achieve could be done so in an instant and in our sleep? It would be real and the waking life would whisper away. All the struggles would mean nothing because when we lay down and shut our eyes, all our phantasies would be under control, lived and tangible. We could all have our successes, all have our moments, and it would be real. For those hours everything would be real.

I would get up still hoping for a new world outside of this, but that never took. I thanked my work for giving me the opportunity to try and make a better one.

I wondered what it would mean for me if the world really did change overnight, and that all my complaints were fixed. What then would be my purpose?

The darkness of society needed me as much as I needed it, to thrive, to survive and have something to rile against. Without it I would have nothing or would turn back and start again, fighting the other way, always assuming the role of underdog.

It absolved me of expectation and seemed always to be the right way.

CHAPTER SEVEN

As time passed, the seasons died with time renewed. The gaunt tree waving at his front windows was beginning to bloom. The small buds of whitish-green pumped out of each branch and opened into the sky. Soon he would have his view obscured by these leaves slowly bursting. The thin branches had always in previous years held many leaves that grew in bunches hanging innocent from beginning, middle and end.

Finally, perhaps, this might end his obsession. He would no longer sit hours at the window, shuffling the cards and mixing them back, trying to find original order, watching as two lives folded together, in that apartment always held fast in his eyes.

The many hours of bending and shuffling had rendered the cards a little more pliable, a little more life in their backs, that they now bent and obeyed his will. The corners were scuffed and cracked from the constant beating together between his fingers. And he kept at it. Cut the pile, handle the decks and hold them close, before blurring them with a hundred cracks, the riffle shuffle, bending them all into an arc and interleaving them down into one another. Immer wieder. Again and again.

With the trees now birthing new life, so too the young man and woman echoed the feeling. Where bookshelves had once been empty, they were now filled with an array of ornaments and decoration. Filled all along the wall and, back there, yet another running beneath holding trinkets and sentimentality.

Yet no books in their third floor nest.

Samstag felt their advance, as the guardian of their relationship, and saw the rooms filled in every corner with every kind of household gadget and adornment. He watched in the cold hollow of his own room as an orangey warmth crept the beige walls, up to the wooden slats of the ceiling.

He had begun to foster the habit of looking up at their third floor apartment from his level, and from the ground, when he occasionally left to pick modest groceries or complete minor assignments, assignments that required the lowest level of empirical data, to keep the authorities from arriving to inspect his health. He would still carry out small freelance procedure to keep the rent settled. But that was all. He had completely lost feeling for his purpose and his work, but this relaxed him. As he found himself closer to the ground, ease set in. He liked to think that at some point he might return to some form of work, that after the long break of self-inflicted solitude, with time to contemplate and recharge, his mind may be fit for renewal, like the blossoming tree that blocked his view.

As spring and summer drew closer, as snow melted into heat, the two in the room afforded Samstag further access into their routine. He noticed, amongst other things, that their television was rarely reflecting black. And he noticed their screen often looked identical to the other screens he could see in adjacent apartments, above and below, channelling the same transmission.

Frequently he could make out the figures on the picture. Though he paid little attention to what they watched, he often noticed a common sinew in the images. And the television flashed different colours, different shades of light, beams that zipped out of the box and at times seemed to illuminate the entire block. They rarely spoke or moved as they sat there under the beams.

Samstag absentmindedly shuffled the two-pile deck.

They would arrive home at differing hours every day. He would feel disappointment, a bitter urgency, if they were not home by nightfall. Or if the lights were out all evening. These were the hours he could best see through the glass.

Before going to bed, she would approach the bedroom window. Samstag would lower his body or move toward a wall where he thought he would most certainly not be seen. He begged her in whispers not to lower the blinds. She opened the window. The top of it leaned inward a few inches; allowing passage to the odour of the street; the sounds of parents walking behind children; of prams pushed and handbags wrestled. Samstag edged closer to the glass as she stood there, as she occasionally ducked out of sight to fix something or other, to make the bed, or to plug in some appliance.

This time, she turned and looked over her shoulder. The man was standing there too, facing the window. They rarely looked out with any intention, but this time they watched and pointed at something.

He quickly dropped down and hid, putting his back against the wall, the chamber in his chest beating fast, the feeling of shame strangling him there squatted in the darkness. His knees up to his cheeks.

The shame of being caught was his deepest concern. Though for him at that moment, it was more a fear of reprisals. For if they caught him, his obsession would be exposed, and possibly pushed further to an unknown limit, his dreary self-loathing sunk deeper, and the reality of his existence dug, to be buried alive.

But he knew that if they caught him, the game would not be up. His method would only become more devious, more cunning, as he sought new ways to observe them in his mania.

In the moments where he came closest to being discovered, the terror of the situation took hold. Whenever they decided to shut the blinds, all of them on every window, in both the visible rooms, he feared that they knew something. That they knew he had been watching them, and now they were frightened.

They themselves now hid from his watchful eye and planned to unearth him, to destroy him. A simple phone call, to the landlord, or to the Metro Polis, would certainly terrify him into some depraved, perverted act. Carried out either against them, or against himself. He could hardly decide which was worse. He did not want to hurt them. But he did not want to torture himself any longer either, he only wanted the simple pleasure of observation.

He was no deviant. He had never used what he saw for anything questionable. Anything repulsive. It was repulsion that made him do it in the first place, he thought. Repulsion at everything else in his mind and his work. Yet he was fully conscious of what may happen if he was sent off the outer edge of mania.

He knew what might happen.

By the time I sat up, every morning at the exact same hour, more papers would be waiting. I went to them with haste, my tasks already set for the day, no other arrangements necessary.

As I began, the morose thoughts backed away. This one, the next one and the last.

Did I smile during this time? I did. I smiled at my work. I smiled at my self. The sacrifice I made of my own mind now had a purpose, I did not have to wither and die alone.

The winter was over. It was heavenly success and spring. I sat back against the wall, delusional and poisonous thoughts filling my vision, my name sliding past a new, closer layer of sight: in large, printed letters like a passing cloud of language, my name. And I imagined the impression I would make on people that once knew me. They would recognise my name and think: Oh, I know him, I always knew he would be something. They would be happy for me or they would be jealous, but nevertheless they would respect me. Or fear me. And my name would be a solid cloud. My name would intimidate them and make me less uncomfortable in my own skin. More layers concealing the truth.

But I wouldn't have to express this. It would be a given. I would have their precious success and it would stifle their days. It would grate on them that I, who was once sucked in and spat out, was now at the top. My face smiled. My mouth smiled, showed teeth.

By then it had gotten to the point where they no longer needed the hood. We were allowed to see what was around us, what was held in those cells. There was a quadrant, a garden between the buildings where nature crowed and aged. Inside, we were timeless. There was only work, our purpose, our lives holed up in security. I saw room upon room, soft horror chambers of rows and machines, desks in the factory of news.

The doors had labels: Military, Foreign, Domestic, Crime, Sport, Culture, Processing and Special Reports. Our chamber was without an official label, but the word DATA was etched in plastic below the window in the door.

The trainees that sat inside were just the same, vacuous and waiting to be filled by the corporation. They would greet you as you walked in. Code. Their eyes alive with lies, never following you any further than the door. The task was too important, or the guest not enough. Sentient drones. With the words pasted along the walls in the new spirit of the age, 'Attain Intellectual Wealth, Forget All but Self', we kept our minds right. We sunk in our warm places, knocking out the templates.

We began to learn more and thrived. New templates evolved, but we never forgot the primers. They were there to stay.

We began tasks of memorisation that seemed to continue through all consciousness and sleep, as when we first began in the mornings tapping out key paragraphs that corresponded to some fictional event, we could recall with ease all of the previous day's teachings down to the smallest detail. Spot checks and exams were forced upon us. Failure meant retaking. Retaking until succeeding. In the age of amnesia we were learning to remember. All the facts, all the knowledge. Facts were sacred. They were indisputable, we assured our selves. Our confidence blossomed in this, the finest of seasons.

When outside all was darkness, black and white, we thrived and climbed upon each other's shoulders. Objective with others, subjective with self. Some trampled their way up to the summit, others left trodden and squished in the heap. We succeeded through the other's failure. Competition: the answer. And for that we gained a grand sense of superiority.

If we were better than these, the cream, then we were surely better than all the rest that lay outside. Duty and honour. And though some became suppressed, depressed, in their position, they were nonetheless gladder for it than when it all began. They too could be victorious. Only a little effort was required. That was little to ask.

We filled the avenues with our conquest.

Those first templates were so deeply ingrained, so driven in stone, that only a severe bolt to the head could possibly displace them. They were natural now. It wasn't only how or what we wrote. It was what we thought. When we finished templates we typed more, thinking in columns, unable to stop. Omitting inconvenient facts, omitting complexity. Our hearts were glad with such proliferation. Features. Stories of success. There were many, the men who made a million. The ones who rose to the top, the ones they could look up to. They were the good students. *Real* success stories. People taught to understand they must fight for themselves and can't rely on others. Self. We looked at ourselves, nodding inside. Yes. We were those success stories too, explaining the world through an objective lens. But we didn't need riches, we were noble, we were above wealth and money. Truth was our currency, and oh how we coveted that prize and any of those who realised they were part of the club, with Us, the winners.

We all fell into line, all into the same stream, forging all the new swords in the fire. A trainee would tighten his neck, and his jaw would loosen. He would throw out an answer, a string of platitudinous words but correct ones. And the class would echo it.

The room reverberated with the feeling of a collective understanding.

Then the rest would follow. Each would take a turn at leading the way, and the others fell in behind. There are 'right' answers. And there are 'wrong' answers. There are 'right' questions, and 'wrong' ones.

Over time we took the grounding we already held in our first languages, to build on it in the new one. The esoteric becoming the familiar. The addled mind converted to a functioning one. Never reverting back to the original thought patterns, we left behind archaic notions of honesty and truth. We became Objective.

We too were creators, freely undertaking work, in association with our colleagues, because of our love of society and humanity. The progressive and creative core of man's existence.

We were proud and gloried. Our heads never dropped.

Thank you, we would say,

Thank you to the Judge and the man in black,

Thank you to the guards, thank you to Metropolis

for the opportunity to make something bigger

and better than ourselves alone

under this democratic sky.

In all possible ways, we had been released.

Metropolis provided me with a new home, just the same as the other interns: a fresh apartment with the latest appliances, a gleaming machine hunkered on an oak desk, for both work and for leisure. It was fitted with a modern kitchen, set under a skylight that stretched across the entire flat and over to the bed. A sheet of ice; the edge of my bubble to the world – that caught rain, and played with snow, singing when the sun shone.

The bed was a magnificent creation, where I dreamt real dreams of work and creativity. Yet I could no longer recall my dreams anymore, the days of work seemed to overlap with my nights of rest, blurring as one.

No matter, I smiled, walking through to the kitchen, across the soft green carpet through to the charcoal tiles around the cooker and the fridge. I pulled out fresh juice, setting down a glass from the cupboard and watched the world awake in me. I sipped at the orange nectar. Days of pen and paper were gone; I had even been given an additional typewriter for recreation.

I looked across at it, watching it lovingly, like a father would a child. I submitted all my work, reams of it, day after day with a genuine smile drawn across my face. Now strangers and friends and enemies alike would read my words and heed what I said, like some sickly authority that they needed.

I downed the rest of the juice and moved over to the news-hub.

And that landlady, and all the ones who had forsaken me. They would learn.

Switching it on, I watched the television reports coming in on the sheet screen, as I flicked the switch on the monitor, never taking my eyes off the moving images. I felt a sudden, cold desolation. A sterile and eerie landscape of nothingness cast between the world and its inhabitants. The barriers had been put up. In there, they fostered that Something inside us wanting to be watched, to be admired. That Something wanting to be noticed. Clashing with that part of us that wants to be ignored. Something there but not quite palpable.

The screens protected us from reality and prevented us from thought. An army of voyeurs bred by the million. Peeping toms behind the keyhole of ego.

But still how I was never disgusted at my self, never bored, always comforted when loneliness and fear began to set in, and all with a flick of a switch, a tap of a button, the back of my seat catching me with such beatific ease.

And then the friendly faces, explaining to me the horrors.

Bombs exploded across the city of <u>Tehran</u> today, as violence erupted once again in the <u>Iranian capital</u>. <u>Spokesmen</u> for the <u>international community</u> condemned the persistent violations of <u>human rights</u> in the region, calling the <u>Iranian</u> government 'amoral and antiquated'.

When I heard the report my head began to shake. Every other week it was the same.

The phone rang.

Sonntag speaking…

OK…

Are you sure?

Right, until when?

Okay. Anything else?

Oh, yes, fine. I'll be there.

Thank you.

Goodbye.

I replaced the handset as my eyes retained their hold on the screen.

The office, shut down again, some inconsistency with our machinery. But an invitation to a speech later this evening. Fine, I would work from home.

I watched the scenes. The Fires, people screaming, hell cries to the sky, more sobbing. They were the unworthy victims of continuing sabotage. They were good people, honest, obedient, why did these extremists resist humanitarian aid with such fervency, and with such ignorance? Did they not understand the *bigger* picture? These attacks were common now, but they never ceased to utterly mortify, and at the same time fascinate, some dark part of my intellect.

I went over to the computer screen and began typing.

The reality and the unreality of it always struck me. We didn't have to imagine what it would be like; our own city had faced the same troubles not long ago. But our government was taking the necessary steps at preventing that from happening again. We were fighting the good fight. Humanitarian intervention wasn't always an easy decision to take, but we had a duty. Social mobility was unlocked not just in the domestic sphere, but the international. Freedom and fairness. Responsibility was there for those who could shoulder it. Equality. Complete egalitarianism was the ideal. Everyone on the same even keel. We could all have our chance in these chambers of opportunity. Ambition and talent were cultivated within enterprise and The Market. I began to write, The Possibility of Greatness. It wasn't just a reversal of definitions, it was all *real* policy, and not only rhetoric as it was before the Progressive Alliance. We protected, that's what we did. Everyone that had something, anything, was going to be protected. Business: The Great Innovator.

I finished the last Word and stood up to stretch, the blood re-entering my limbs after the surge to the brain. I clicked send and mailed my latest piece over.

It went straight up and was picked up across the nationwide press.

I cracked my back and my neck, satisfied.

Hopping into bed, I crawled into the skylight's sunbeams, basking in the morning rays. The bed was big enough for three, I grinned. Though it had been a long time since I had a woman, I felt the calm release of soon being able to tell a girl: Yes, I'm a reporter. For Metropolis. Yes, I'm going places, we're going places. And seeing her face soften and draw nearer, a hand on my lap, and leaning in with her chest, welcoming, inviting me into her night-like beauty.

I leant back at the head of the bed, white, plain, modern and minimalist, the style of the hour. She whispered in my ear, her hand sliding up to my thigh: Where d'you wanna take me? I smiled, a wide Cheshire to my self. Her red lips smooth and caressing, her chest heaving irregular, I took her in my arms and into my bed, there, all empty, stretching out the legs of my imagination.

I had a letterbox, filled every morning, greetings and newsletters from Metropolis – all the latest updates. I thought back to the days of my rejection-filled post box in the bedsit. It swarmed over me, the melancholy and loathing of my life seeping back in. Flashes of horror better forgotten, ignored. And in other envelopes I had the dearest hand-typed notes to me. Acceptance slips for all my work. *Thank you for your recent contributions. Your work is extremely important to us. You have found your place here and we look forward to reading more.* Validation in an envelope. Validation in an inbox.

I pasted the slips up around my workstation. I gleamed at them whenever I had a moment of doubt looking out the window at the beggars jittering by, ants far below. I had no need to leave my apartment much. The world outside was grim and unwelcoming, perhaps even unreal at times. It was a bleak place where men got killed in the confusion, or killed themselves by accident.

Here I was sure of my self, and sure of my work, my purpose. I wallowed there in my great responsibilities, my glory of bringing the world to the people, protecting them from the threats outside.

It was evening. I moved off on my way to a speech given by the new Managing Editor, my mentor Stearns, at Lawrence Hall. I stepped onto the train, after walking down from my apartment building, in a district where mostly enforcement officers and some ministry workers resided.

I reflected. I had spent the first part of the evening doing what I usually did.

Everyday I looked up the work I had published on the home machines we were given. I read them over, analysing my choice of words, the unified message I delivered and saw as a virtue. It was good. Not once did a word seem out of place. Every choice a victory. The language flowed and the meaning was tempered, instructive to anyone that read it. I beamed with a visceral triumph that I was really doing it, what I had been born for. This could make me immortal.

I sometimes read the comments on my work, they were overwhelmingly positive. I felt a profound joy at this acceptance. I must have been like them, in a way, but still superior. Yes, still superior. I was telling them what they should be thinking and what they should be doing. With their time, with their thoughts, with their donations. These people, with plain names like Peter, who looked up to me and had enjoyed my work and they were grateful I did it. This gave me a justification, a righteousness that continued to build in me.

Now and then I scanned over some negative comments, left mostly by obvious extremists. I mostly ignored them but for some inexplicable reason they greatly affected me. They were often childish and simply could not understand the lucidity I was delivering on complicated issues.

Reference CAS-908182

Thank you for your letter. We appreciate your concern.

We understand that you believe *Metropolis* in general is biased in its reporting on the (blank) situation towards the (blank) perspective.

We can assure you that we are committed to covering events in the (blank) region in a scrupulously impartial, fair, accurate, balanced, independent manner. The aim of our news reports is to provide the information across our programming in order to enable viewers and listeners to make up their own minds; to show the reality of a situation and provide the forum for debate, giving full opportunity for all viewpoints to be heard. We are satisfied that this has been the case in respect of our reporting of the (blank). Nevertheless, I recognise you may continue to hold a different opinion about the (blank)'s impartiality.

Please be assured that I've registered your obvious strong feelings about our coverage on our audience log. This is a daily report of audience feedback that's circulated to many *Metropolis* staff, including members of the *Metropolis* Executive Board, channel controllers and other senior managers.

Thank you once again for taking the time to share your views with us.

Metropolis felt it important we gave the buyer an opportunity to have their say, even the ones who were terribly misinformed or extreme in their ignorance.

We never took too much notice of the negatives, as writers we felt the editors up there, somewhere, were taking notice of our great solidarity in the face of such negativity. It didn't matter to them that our narrative began to bend toward the middle road, alienating the zealots. At least it wasn't mediocre. When we argued our points back with the masses, it gave them a feeling that they had choice in their product, that they were a part of it. It was enough for us.

The more readers, the more advertising, the more advertising, the more money, the more money, the bigger the message. It was a mantra the editors repeated and it made me nod ferociously.

Every other news agency joined us on this quest for a democratic veneer in media. Everyone now paid *us* for the data we gave to them. We were overcoming what froze Socrates when it came to the printed word, we were creating a dialogue. The image our writing portrayed was not of petrified orthodoxy, it was just part of a conversation.

Democracy is the root of our service.

This is how our Managing Editor began his address. Democracy for some, a voice in my head retorted. My brow furrowed and I cast the strange thought aside. Butterfly back to Slug.

Ladies and Gentlemen. I wish to thank you heartily for your kind sympathy and appreciation. He paused. We are not deceiving ourselves in the fact, of which you must be aware, that we have achieved no modest feat. One should, in such a situation, be diffident. But self-assertive. And so, in that vein, I will concede, some measure of credit may be due to me for our first steps in certain new directions. The ideas I advanced have been a triumph; the forces and elements of the centrist demagoguery and ideological Right have been conquered, and greatness achieved, through the co-operation of many able men. Some of whom, I am glad to say, are present this evening. Creators, writers, investigators, polemicists and enforcers have done their share, until a wholesale revolution has been wrought in the transmission and transformation of news.

While we are of course elated with the results achieved so far, we must continue pressing on, inspired with the hope and conviction that this is just a beginning, a forerunner of further and still greater accomplishments.

Ladies and Gentlemen, we stand at the constant dawning of a New Age, said Stearns, standing up ahead of the audience. His hair shook as he spoke, thick on top and swept back at the sides, with a fashionable gray-white beard, giving the impression of a man with little time for grooming. A savage intellectual, the eyes of objective honesty and truth looking up and down, from notes to audience. The sweat twinkled at the tip of his forehead, his shirt open revealing more perspiration. As he spoke, a sweeping English accent booming from the speakers, the hall swarmed with adulation, great writers and great communicators sitting side by side. I was amongst them, in the fifth row, where I had muscled in early, having taken my seat a whole hour before the conference began. This is it, I thought. One day, I'll be up there, and all these faces will look to me for the way, the answer, the Reason.

Stearns spoke to us: We must invert totalitarianism. Fight it on every corner, to expose unethical practices, illegal behavior, and wrongdoing within the corrupt corporations and oppressive regimes wherever they may be: in Asia, the former Soviet bloc, Sub-Saharan Africa, the Middle East. Or even here, at home.

It's our job. Our duty, to keep the people interested spectators in the game of life, and politics, to direct the great beast of humankind toward greater realisation of the self and democracy.

It is the success of our system that we can all be proud of, because each and every one of us is a sentinel along the great wall.

For hope. For posterity. And for prosperity.

Our work must encourage them to participate, to vote, encourage them to make decisions of real import. Not question the system, for the system is indestructible, we know that now. For without it, where would we be?

It is not *anarchy* mankind needs. It is social responsibility, for each other and for ourselves. Our selves... (He pondered for a moment.)

We *educate* the sorry and the ignorant, the uninitiated, into understanding the real gratitude they ought to feel when their leaders stand among them.

We are building *political* support here, not *majority* support. For those that cannot best judge their own interests, we are to guide them, take them by the hand and lead them down the gentle path.

We must *manage* this system with *skill* and *dexterity*, build it and feed it with our continuing commitment.

Manage, that is all we can do in this life.

CHAPTER EIGHT

Though he did not really believe they had ever caught him in the act, on many occasions Samstag thought they had seen something. Some odd figure. Someone watching. On the occasions when he was given to these thoughts, he resolved that he had good reason for suspecting it. One of their heads might turn and look right in his direction. He would swear to himself they had connected with him.

Yet he was afraid of this.

He could see only their silhouettes most of the time, and could therefore never be certain what their eyes saw exactly. Samstag would often imagine what they might see in their vision. Yet it was most peculiar to him, the idea that looking from their window they may see him, sat there, a black figure in more blackness. Still, silent. He felt the sure horror of what they may feel, in the knowledge that they had been watched so closely and for so long. They would put it all together instantly. All the strange coincidences. The omnipresent figure in the window.

But really, despite the length of time, he had only seen very little of their lives. He had only once seen them make love, though he knew they were doing it more often. Only out of sight. That time he did see them though, was toward the beginning of his habit, where the current impulse was merely a curiosity. He thought that this event might even have been the trigger for his swimming down into the depths of this suspicious behaviour.

He also thought that this occasion would be the one they would come to feel most violated by, most livid with, if they ever came to identifying his transgression. He imagined their sheer trembling. But he often thought she, out of the two of them, would be bothered least.

Samstag imagined that others along his side of the street, who could see the same scenes, were watching too. And Samstag felt sometimes that she was putting on a show for all of them, all of the desperate tenants along the city street, by their windows, in yellow light. Samstag would sometimes whisper this to himself as he watched, nose against the glass, as she moved seductively and erotically, after a shower or before getting dressed, to and fro across the living room, and the bedroom, a wet towel on her head or an immodest nightgown gliding behind her, by the curtain half-drawn.

He imagined the troglodytes in the neighbouring apartments intruding on the same scene and, being unable to suppress the primal urge, thrusting into their fists until completion. The thought made him sick and weak.

For she was his, and must remain unspoiled. Though

nothing more than an experiment in truth.

But he could not help notice the craving build during his watch.

The urge for her to undress, to be unknowingly naked before his eyes only, and silent before the earth.

She was the wearer of nothing, but he could never have her.

But this man did, and despite feeling no envy for this man's position, Samstag seemed to rather despise him. His every action boiled a muddy fear in him, that his animal violence would one day come down on Samstag and delete him and his existence from history.

Samstag was not sure whether this was *really* the fear that gently choked him. He urged the thought of what it might be at times when it struck him, in the evenings as he watched the man moving about the flat, where he would eventually find his seat again, in the same place, and rest.

CHAPTER NINE

Stearns' words glowed inside me. Masterful, I thought. Catching a glimpse of my self starry-eyed staring up at the spotlit stage, the dark curtain and the Metropolis insignia hanging over. All flush and crisp. I cringed a little at my own monomania.

I looked around quickly to see if I had been caught peering so adoringly at the host. No one had taken any notice, they were busy themselves, their eyes glinting like glass on stone, eyeballs streamed into the same stage lights, clapping furiously red during each calculated pause. The same waves vibrating in all of us.

This life, I reflected, looking at my colleagues, some grand feeling soaring up inside me, swarming my emotions, was what I had tried and failed to achieve in my previous lifetime, writing to them from behind walls, never confronting them but working covertly and in secrecy, ashamedly. I felt light and free, as if I could at any moment burst up into space.

In our free and democratic society, where sometimes opportunities must be thrust upon men, as they were upon me, we cannot allow for apologetic attitudes. Take them and show them what is best, so every morning they can thank their protectors, as I thanked mine.

I was part of it, a notch on the great club of humanity, spreading it to the confused masses down in the street. Oh, how the beggar would thank me if he only knew. And how I, as a beggar, would have thanked them before, had I known what I have since learnt. And wouldn't the beggar see the beauty in life, the sheer wonder of love and creativity, as we look on at our leaders setting the example? They wouldn't need to drudge or slave against change, if only they let the grip loosen and let it happen! I could tell them now! For I was part of that great and fair society finally, that great society in which none of us can fail!

I quickly went home.

I tore through time.

I sat at my desk.

Politics wasn't a shadow that cast itself upon our fair society; it was the golden flower that we all trampled in times of desperation, times of need. The symbol of (blank), of hope, of rebirth, of _change_. But it was just a word, 'politics'. Though when we looked, it spoke directly to our hearts, as a means of bringing us together, bringing us unity.

But there was no such thing as unity there; it was more like complacency, or a way of giving in to someone else's interests. No, that's negative thinking. The World will not become better with cynicism. I no longer needed to question, to think what the purpose of my work was, though I knew it only to be true and good. I only needed to accept and be grateful for the work as it's own end. In these moments, I felt ashamed of my self that I had stolen from others, others who worked hard for the joy of work. But I could recover my pride, and theirs, by doing great work for the advancement of our fair society. I had conquered *Mediocrity*. And we had won the *Hearts and Minds* of our people.

They had unveiled a glorious monument outside our apartment building, commemorating the deaths of (*thousands*) during the (blank) War, the fifth such monument in our district. We arrived for the grand opening. There it stood, the singular monolithic structure, (*black*) and (*matte*), growing up from the ground, with a splatter of (*green*) surrounding its base.

We looked it up and down, the Great Flag waving above us, and we applauded the young man who conceived such a wondrous thing and we shook his hand and applauded again and then we went back to our homes smiling and chattering, how great that someone had done something with such conviction, such faith, but still smiling more that we had witnessed such fantastic freedom at the privilege of having our (*liberty*) bought and paid for by the (*brave*) soldiers, the (*brave*) men and women, bought and paid for with lives, and spirit. I heard the Leader's voice in my head: The Brave Men and Women, who sacrifice themselves daily for our safety, our freedom and our peace. My mind applauded.

My education was a great instruction. Dead was the anarchic mindset I had professed to, during what seemed whole epochs previous. There was no more wisdom in solitude, in individuality. I needed people, and the people needed me. We would join in hand and mind and word and purpose. It was a duty that I couldn't back down from now.

Music blared from the headphones jacked into the handheld devices in our pockets; everywhere we were offered something for nothing. Upper management seeping into the everyday experience.

No time to think, and no need to, we would regiment a time and a place for that. We put up with strobe advertising, constantly moving images, unapologetic attacks on our physiology, in return for what we wanted.

It wasn't much to ask for.

CHAPTER TEN

The trees were now heavy with leaves and he strained his eyes struggling to see through them. A gnawing mania grew inside Samstag as the difficulties forced upon him mounted, the nature of that tree's life cycle taunting him. He swayed with it when the breeze blew, directing his vision between the branches as it shifted through his gaze. It was stubborn, he thought, a grave irritation. He planned for its removal.

Light faded.

She had been standing by the window only for a moment when Samstag returned to his perch. He had the cigarettes now in hand. He puffed while he observed. She turned slightly and revealed a distended stomach. A growing bump.

Another inside her.

Getting to work was always automatic, always the same. I got up, dressed, grabbed my bag full of notes and paper and headed toward the station. I read some of the papers, or I listened to something on the headphones, to kill time until I arrived at my purpose.

We studied the other newswires; we looked at where they were going wrong. They had a unity as we did, but the people simply couldn't get behind it as much as ours. We offered them something else. Something esoteric as if hidden by the world in its confusion, we made it clear, giving them what they already knew to be true.

I walked in through the glass doors, the light shining through from clouds to make everything sheen and reflected in dull whites. The scent. Her odour hung in the aorta.

Hello, Sir. The receptionist greeted me as I walked in.

Hi. I didn't know her name, but I mumbled something inaudible trying to recall, to guess what it might be, but still kept walking trying to suppress the scene that familiar odour brought with it.

She looked into my eyes smiling, a small thing she was sat there, humble, a smile fading into uncertainty as I nodded, not knowing where to put the words. Communication was still a discomforting thing, when it was spoken. I was awkward, and it was noticeable in my steps, to the point that my movements, as if joining my observer in watching my self walk, became stifled and strange little kicks.

I asked my self.

Think of something to say.

I kept moving, still making eye contact for a duration that had entered 'unnerving', and wanting to say a word of greeting though I still moved on past her desk. How are things? I would have asked, polite, personable, that would be enough. A warm smile that showed understanding, amiability. Empathy. What did she expect? I was focused on the job; I had to look as if I knew what I was doing. No, I knew what I was doing, mending the broken soul, replacing parts. But in fact, I only knew *where* I was going.

The scent again. Sticky.

She stepped out of her self-imposed exile, coming to me, from the adjoining room. She waited in the doorway.

How do I smell?

Beautiful.

Thank you. I just showered.

I know.

She glided across and slid in alongside my right flank. She turned to something not inside this room. She spoke over her shoulder full of hair:

I have something to tell you.

I could not believe her tone. Twisted. Obvious. As if lifted from some toilet fiction.

I watched my self walk past and nodded again, blurted something incomprehensible and just kept on moving. The sweat pouring down my brow. Kill the memory. Can't even make small with the help. The belly hollow. Visions of mutilated limbs climbing the walls of my conscience. I needed some heavy distraction, an innocent hobby for the mind.

I got into the lift and pressed the button, waiting for the door to close. Close. *Close.*

She had turned back to her desk and looked up again as the doors were closing. *Close.* She could see me still watching her as the lift shut its doors and moved up to the fifth floor.

Her long black hair shone, sucking in light from the sheets of sun shot through. The frame of her glasses winked, a glimmer. I shook my head swimming in disappointment at not being able to connect with her, with anyone, even in a small way that might put her at ease, put my self at ease. Put us all in the safe place. Miniscule moments like this could put my day off at an angle irretrievable, and would follow me through the rest of the long hour. A layer peeled off, one closer to the truth.

I decided then, I would stay put in the office until she would surely be gone, by 5.30 pm, I assumed. Then at least we could both avoid the strange and uneasy feeling I forced into both of us, both of our trembling shells.

No, she wasn't the same, she was confident, she had an air about her, a musk that exuded positive charm. She been through, or possibly even seen, fictional representations of the things I had done, the days and nights against the wall. Why couldn't I wear the mask straight and rigid, pretend it all, believe it easily, to be confident?

Arrogant in my purpose. She could smell it on me, my self-loathing, my misdirected spirit, but I went up in the shaft and came out at the flat angles of the office, feeling at ease again.

The possibility of her eyes recognising herself in mine now just a dissolving apparition.

The belly filled and the intestines jutted.

I hoped she wouldn't be there the next day or the one after, or if I came in early, before her shift started, we could avoid the danger of being caught again. Hopefully she wouldn't pre-empt this manoeuvre and thwart my avoidance.

What life was this, that had me avoiding contact with discomforting elements, why could it not be pushed to the back, with my feigned personality at the fore? The mask over the mask over the mask over the mask.

This was mere *existing*, not *living*, and the kind of comment you'd read on some sophomore's t-shirt, after he's discovered Nietzsche, and I, unable to communicate and say: Hi how are you? Busy down here? The blood rush drank me in. Yeah things are pretty hectic up there, a lot going on, I'm sure you know, you have to deal with all the calls, don't you? How about a drink tonight? You can come around to mine for a few or we can hit a bar? I'm a writer, yeah. Uh huh. Not too bad. It's got its perks.

I'm glad I didn't say that, too forward, forced, she would see it coming, see what I wanted, or at least what it was that I was supposed to have wanted. What's your name? Is it too late to ask, I left it too long didn't I? Oh no it's alright. Imaginary conversations were smooth. The real thing was awkward, I wanted them just to say the easy thing, what I expected them to say in a tight squeeze such as that.

No, it's okay, she might say, I like you, I'd love to have a drink with you some time, it wouldn't be weird. Oh, ha, yes thank you for that. She wouldn't say anything like that, she could tell by just looking at my eyes that I was strange, possibly even dangerous, she wouldn't let me get too close to her. She told me all this with her questioning eyes that watched me and judged me, her eyebrows there, her glasses glinting like sun on stone.

Why did she do that? Did she know what she was doing to me? That she cringed my insides with just a look out of the side of her face.

An Axe flashed.

No she knew, she must have thought it was a possibility at least. She was delicate, I thought. Delicate and aching to be touched. Or was she already seeing someone. Could she be in a relationship?

The thick air of burning filled my nostrils. Maybe I could get to her at an office party? Yes, there was the centenary soon; she would be there. She would have to be. Every employee would have to at least show their faces, show their support. I could save face that way. Approach her then dismiss her. Keep hold of honour, of status. The mask behind the face. Though maybe she didn't believe in the Cause, maybe she had other things going on, more fun, more exciting, she wasn't wallowing in nausea and despair at having to talk to people one on one, she didn't need the shield of rank to protect her thoughts and behaviour.

Oh, god.

My days were filled by fear even of others. But it was the fear that kept me conscious. The craze that never turned the inward out. Poison coursed its way through the ducts and condemned all hope to damnation.

How I would sing when all life would fall down on its knees.

CHAPTER ELEVEN

The tree played upon his weakness. It teased him through the day but especially at night. There were goings-on that he could not quite fathom, not quite make out. He cursed the tree and thought to himself: Autumn will put an end to your arrogance.

But he could not wait any longer for the passing seasons. Spring had only just begun. Wait until autumn, he repeated to himself. No. He could not.

Day faded further until streetlamps warmed the street with plastic orange light. That night the rain fell thick from a dark mass looming overhead. The indifferent sky dripping from black-gray to transparent. He felt it drip within his skull. He made strides for the toolbox in the bottom of his wardrobe. Covered with dust. He opened its lid and removed the Axe. As he looked out of the window at the branches and the leaves that so teased him, his finger ran unknowingly along the blade. The tip of his long index split, without bleeding, as it reached the edge of the Axe's toe. He felt none of the pain.

He returned to the window.

His hand now rested under the Axe's cheek. He wondered if there was some other way. There was no other way.

He thought maybe lightning might strike it. He could not seriously believe that, or consider it a solution. He decided he must down it with his own strike. His own earthly fire. The earthly fire that had downed all else in this world, he reasoned.

He lifted his coat from the floor, folded by the wall where it spread across discarded cigarettes butts on a laminate floor. He did not once relinquish the Axe. He glanced again into the sky and wondered whether the rain might stop. When the clouds might serve him. Perhaps it is better that it rains tonight, he thought. There would be fewer out on the street to see him work.

He made his way down the staircase. He moved quietly on the balls of his feet, gripping the handle while he buttoned the coat to the neck. He prayed no one would see him carrying on this way. He imagined the peepholes that faced out onto the stairway darkening with the eyes of strangers watching him skulk down.

He made a strained effort to silence his steps completely.

It could not be done. An old building, an old stairwell. It would creak out its age.

He came to the bottom and moved past the post boxes. He moved past his name and the next and all of his neighbours'. He realised he had not blinked since leaving the flat. He stood at the precipice, opened the large door and looked then at the small set of four steps lead-ing down. He blinked.

The world at the end of the steps barely visible. The rain spattered against the panels of the door, the glass opened inward. He felt it on his face. He looked up and reached out the Axe. He let the rain fall along its length.

In the darkness the hatchet was black, the sky above it a lighter hue. He looked along the horizon he had formed, the Axe on the sky. He felt a bubbling nausea, as if he were caught in someone else's sick dream.

Taking the axe-head back into his hand, he ducked his head and ran, over the cobble steps, around to the right and down the small alley.

Dead and soaked cigarettes ran under his shoes.

He paused, before the edge of the building fully re-vealed him. He looked up at the building across. The blinds were up and blank faces looked out. He could see their heads through the shifting leaves. He counted. This time, the faces, on the fourth floor.

The light of the room, the wooden slats that made their ceiling. A view he had never before been able to truly appreciate. A small procession of cars made their way through the rain, their windshields swaying. The cobblestone under the tyres reminded him of some far away weekend. Faint memories. The cars hummed away, faint symphonies held within the glass.

The faces were gone again. He looked at the rest of

the building's façade, the changing light that glimmered out of darkness from the inner plasma. All the living rooms in the column resonated the same harmonious frequency, the same channel. His mouth opened, he gazed at the minor spectacle.

He lost track of time.

The weight of the Axe began to tell. He lowered it to his side, its head resting on the stone with a glint. He surveyed the building and watched. He could not do it yet.

I went straight to my office and shut the door, dropping the blinds down and shutting them all out of sight, so I could take a moment to breathe. The smell still in my nostrils. The data bodies were out there tapping. I had comfort of a momentary disconnection at least, locked up in the box. A small promotion up from the drones, now the *Data Editor* writing the templates for the upstarts to get through. Quick and undeserved. No, I had worked for this, I had sought no favours.

(INT.)

What is it?

I went this morning.

(EXT. OFFICE - NIGHT)

I fumbled through their templates, neat piles laid carefully on the edges of their desks, and I went over them, my limbs aching, looking for minor indiscretions. There were few. They were trained well, no doubt. I eyed them, opening the door having now recovered slightly, but still reeling a little.

Keep it up, I said.

I looked to the clock. Still a few more to get done before lunch.

They looked at me, turning their necks and nodding, then turning back to the screens. Yes, sir. One of them, speaking for the others.

The sound of the flesh hitting the keys and the keys hitting the plastic jittered up out of every one of their systems. Automatons, I thought. Man reverts to automatic. Always to automatic, when the slick and oiled sinews begin to crank. Must remember that one.

I went back to my desk and lifted some papers, looking over a few leaves, the door open, always the door open, don't close it, even if you want to sit there ashamed of yourself. Someone would have noticed the door being shut earlier, someone will have to come and have a word. Oh, god.

I sat at my desk praying no one would come. I pulled up some documents and began working the Data into the templates, filing them and then posting them out to the News section. I suddenly understood the word *breakdown* and suddenly it felt inevitable.

The data matched the corresponding blanks and I put the figures in where there was a blank, a name where there was a blank, a place where there was a blank, and it went on 'til we had some solid news. Hard facts and hard news. *Facts are sacred. The facts don't lie.*

The facts tell the story. Pick the right facts and print those.

Tell the story. Tell the facts.

Oh, god.

But we were actors. And actors aren't real people. Human, yes, but not real people. Morose vagabonds in the twilight of a reborn empire. Remember that, maybe.

(INT.)

I don't know how you could do this. We spoke about this and now.

Now.

The hair on her shoulder stayed still though her head moved. Her face contorted. The words flew out as if in bubbles and the bubbles popped into my eyeballs and the moisture settled on my cheeks.

(EXT. OFFICE - NIGHT)

I left the office building through the rear exit, the grip of nausea clawing at my throat. A long day of it. Holding back the creeping of history. Taking me down, gradually, not allowing me to think. Strangling any hope of a breath. Even the machine-like method in which I downed glassfuls of water worked toward no end. I fuelled my self toward work as my purpose. This purpose of striving to uphold *liberty* and all the *values* instilled in me that, even since an early age, had been inculcated to the point now where I found my self expounding them for every one else's benefit. They had been latent, these feelings before, whereas now they had become kinetic, throwing out of me through my words and thoughts, translated onto the printed page for others to indulge. I had indulged my self for so long. Much longer than most, I felt. But now it was fixed. It was fixed, I told my self.

I felt my self crumbling back toward some earlier craving. The towers of eyes and glass leaned in and watched my pitiful madness curl tightly into rage. All earlier feelings of reason and goodness wallowed in. I believed it had been strength.

The weakness overtook my knees, overtook my hands and a sour odour of decay dulled my senses. There had been many times I had cursed death for taking too long, singing over the hills and the trees forever missing me. Where was it tonight? Why pass my door? Mark me, I screamed. Mark my eyes and swing your blade. The devotion of the Devil breathed in someone else's throat and blew out into the world. I inhaled! What devils had been put to the wind, and what demons had been put into mine. I was delirious with it. What fiendish disorder had I already seen, what memories had been left, and which forgotten?

My body and my mind were shipwrecked.

I hooked along a torn rope on which nothing could balance, but only the inevitability of falling either side. Each side the same, the same consequence. Not by choice or by value, but by arbitrary disgust at the loss of nature, of mystery. Some faith would relieve me. Some true faith. Yes, I had chosen my belief.

No. It had chosen me. As all great beliefs must.

There was only a single truth, and I was following it now. Truth. Let it wash over this, let it fall from the sky, dive in to the ocean's walls.

Erode spirit, erode life.

Bring to it this feeling. The feeling of death for rebirth. Bring to it something lasting, something eternal.

Bring to it the last glimmers of primitive existence, then burn them away.

Then what remains are the crystals of truth.

IRIS IN
BLACK

CHAPTER TWELVE

The street was awash with the filth and the grime that the rain had wrung out of it. The Axe, rested against the wall now, no longer in his hands, stood and waited for a master. He breathed in, drawing his chest up to his neck, letting it out slowly with a trembling.

The rain would not let up. He stood there soaked. By now probably even unable to hold the weapon with any meaningful grip. But he tried.

He lifted it silently, the rain gathering at the eave and dripping wide drops down onto the arm of his coat. This irritated him.

The Axe rose with fervency and moved closer to its point of impact. The handle, straight, untrue. Gripped at the throat. Another hand held it on the shoulder.

His heavy blade cuts through the rain, and the humid air breaks into the skin of the trunk. Four or five inches deep. The strong blow shakes it from root to tip and from the tip back down through the blade, the handle, and the hands. The left hand grips its belly, tight for accuracy and comfort. The rain runs over the eye and the cheek, clearing off all splinters.

The Axe swings and shakes the tree again, this time

beneath the first blow, making another incision of four inches. A third frenzied swing strikes through the bark, leaves shake, dripping collected rain loose and random. The thump and the rustling again, for the fourth and fifth time, starts to weigh the tree slowly down to its side.

He hears tyres on cobblestone and looks to his left and sees the beam of a car coming along the avenue. He wrenches the Axe, now eye-deep in the trunk, out of the tree.

But it can't be moved. The head remains buried.

He decides quickly that the rain will wash off any fingerprints, and resolves that he could not be a suspect. How could one want to destroy a thing of such beauty, something to be proud of, particularly right outside one's home? It would be unthinkable.

He ran back down the soaked alley, the interrogation in his head, leaping up the four steps, sprinting past the empty post boxes and up the stairs.

He fumbled for the key, nearly dropping it, turning around as he picked out the correct one for his door. He sees a peephole darken. An eye behind it.

But the key doesn't fit. He pushes it harder but the metal only scratches the lock and refuses entry. He lays his palm against the door and begins forcing it, again and again leaning all of his slight weight behind the push. Only the door's weak hinges allow any give. He runs upstairs to the next floor and tries that one. No luck. He thinks to go back down then thinks of the darkened peephole. The eye of it blinking. He slaps the door panels in frustration, letting dust fall into his eyes. He curses, rubs them, glasses in hand, the edge of the frame rubbing against his skull as he picks out the foreign bodies.

The next floor. The same result. Each floor as if repeating: Peepholes darkening in question to the frenzy. He spins on his heel and looks down the stairwell. A hand on the banister. Two hands. Three hands. A stomp of bootsteps. Flash of steel. Floorboards giving as much as they could manage before splintering under the weight of the charging uniforms.

He screams a little and runs upward to the top floor and fumbles for the key.

It slips from his grasp and clangs onto the wood.

The boots stop.

Silence.

Breathing.

He kicks in the door.

PART FIVE

Iris Out

CHAPTER ONE

The following day, there was a knocking at my door. The sound of the beating of elbow on wood, the handle rattled a little loose, the hinges shaking with each blow.

From the other side a voice told me it had something to say, some questions to ask, and I let it in out of politeness; there was nothing he could tell me. As it opened he caught me looking at his hand and then at mine again. Habit.

Thanks, he said as he came in, lowering his head as he walked past. Just like mine, your place.

Yeah I think they're all the same.

Probably right.

I looked around as if I had never been in this place before, new and unfamiliar. I shut the door. My door.

Come in then. How've you been? I circled round with some small talk, instead of directly asking the reason for his unscheduled visit. My training had given me tact. Empathy.

Not so good. I haven't been too well the last couple weeks.

Oh, why? I suddenly sounded concerned, caring. Empathy. Oh, god.

Things going over in my mind. Going over things in my mind.

Don't let it get to you. Remember your purpose, keep at it. I said.

Yeah, but it's… difficult. He said.

If it's getting too much just take a break. They'll understand. Just put it to them in writing and you'll get a couple of days off work, no problem. You could even go into recruitment. I hear that's good banter. My voice trembled a little. The amount I was talking unnerved me. I had not spoken for that long in a long time. I shuddered some more for effect.

Maybe.

There are plenty of us to cover your work, don't worry. There are uncountable amounts of eager trainees in Data. Just like we once were. And always more coming in. I show teeth.

Now look at us.

What do you mean? I said. I could see the strain in his eyes, he was becoming disillusioned. I had seen it before, the fade, the fatigue, the grit of colour diluting around him. There was no cure for it. If he started off down this road, there'd be no return. I would have to report him. Code, I could hear. Code.

Have you ever looked out of the train? I mean, on your way to work? Have you seen their faces down there? I know you, you must've seen them.

What do you mean, who are you talking about? Every-one looks focused. All on the way to work. I said. Or just tired, you know. I smiled. Too much of the ol' drink, eh? (I motioned a drinking person and nearly got away with the charade.)

No, not the workers. They're fine. They have some-thing to believe, they can forget the rest. For better or worse. I'm talking about the homeless. Thousands out there. Their feet scratch the ground, their eyes searching my face for charity.

Ignore them. I said. Just ignore them.

I can't. How can I? In the city, the ones begging on their knees, all they see are greedy morons. Fat faces flash-ing past. More labels on these, on these shopping bags, than feet of passers-by. No one even gives them a look. Out of fear. Out of disgust. Or recognition, I don't know. But I've seen it. And one. He asks me for a cigarette. A simple thing. From one to another. And what do I say? I tell him: No. I tell him: No, I don't have any cigarettes. As I stand there blithely smoking one. He looked down. I feel sick with myself.

They're lazy, these homeless. I said, forcefully. Self-righteous. I was once like them, I know how it is. They choose to be that way.

You? What do you mean you were once like them?

Before I began training. I was a vagrant. Yessir. How strange it sounds to voice those words. The worst of the scum, I was. I stole, I thieved. I thought my self a poet. Ha! But that was long before I joined, long before I learnt anything. Or unlearnt everything, I genuinely can't remember which. I let out a laugh, though the situation didn't ease despite having my teeth bared to the air of the room.

But I saw you when you first came in for training. You had all the right papers, all the right documents, identification. You were certainly no bum. You were even wearing a tie.

I'm not quite sure what you mean. I said.

You had a suit on, and shiny bright shoes. We met when you came in for interview. I was there. I shook your hand. Don't you remember any of this?

I'm really still not quite sure what you're talking about. I was taken in by force. I rebelled, but I soon saw the best in it. Code and all that. You know.

By force? He stared deep into my face and I felt my flesh melting away. Code? He muttered.

Yes, the hood, the arrest. By force. Come off it, you know what I'm talking about. I said.

No one is taken by force. He edged forward, looking concerned. What are you talking about Sonntag? You were glad to join. You said you would do anything for the cause.

Oh yes, after a while, I was glad all right. I was delighted when I really learnt what was going on.

He paused and looked at me before he spoke again.

He wore on his face a profoundly puzzled expression, as if devoid of evolution, reversed to Ape encountering Man. Staring into mine as if searching for the answer that I held in my eyes.

I know what I saw. He said.

I know what I saw. I said.

He glanced out of the window and exhaled.

Never mind. He said finally. That isn't the reason why I've come to speak to you.

Quite. I said. I'm sure it isn't.

Yes, it's something far more pressing. Something serious.

Go on.

He looked up and breathed in heavily, picking out the words, his eyes held on the skylight, not looking beyond the glass.

I didn't know whom else I could come to. Because of your history, I thought you might help me. I thought you could help me.

My history? I'm not sure what you mean.

You've dealt with kidnappings before. You wrote that series for the O Press. I did some research last night. Whatever happened to those people? The ones that got kidnapped.

Oh. I sat back and thought, glancing at the blank screen. Nothing, they still haven't turned up yet, I believe. We didn't do any more work on that after the series, you know. Something else came up. I said.

And the kidnappers? Were any of those taken in? He said.

No, I believe not. I looked back into his face. Why do you ask?

I think I've found one of them.

I sat forward. Who? What do you mean you've found one of them?

I've been watching her. Well, I mean, I know what you're thinking. But I didn't have anything to do with it.

Go on. I said. I leaned back. The arms of the chair wrapping around.

It was a while back. She was living in the building across.

I lit the cigarette. Puffed. Then laid it down on the groove in the ashtray.

She's living with me now. Samstag said.

I crossed my right leg over the left. Who is?

The victim. The woman. She is my partner. She is my...

To take my eyes off him a moment, to dull the sweep of his voice, I glanced at the cigarette burning. The tremble.

The sirens in my ears. The sirens in the window. The anguish.

I sat forward and smiled.

DISSOLVE

CHAPTER TWO

It took me a while, but I saw that one coming. I knew their tricks. What else could they have planned for me, except my ultimate downfall? They drew the twigs from the bush. Who was it? The Old Man and *her*, certainly. But who else? Joe the Knife. Hearing it in my head now, his story seemed just a cover. Surely not. Had he given it all up to fund their stunt that day at the protest? Preposterous. But his soft hands.

And Stearns. I realised, he had drawn me in closer for a reason. It almost made sense. The money. Where could they have gotten the money otherwise? They already had insiders. And they had committed, fully.

The Knife had lost his family, everything. Hadn't he?

Nothing seemed certain but the fact that they were using me.

They took their twigs, snapped the ends and made them even. They sent the world down the hole and me with it. Swirling the edges, tripping the line. I drained and swam around the end of time with the dirt and the filth of cosmic failure.

The fear of failure rather than the glory of success, it ate at me. The competitive sieve I'd been fed through, dripping with the built hopes of many, forsaken by man against man. Medium against mediocre. Mother against mothered. Mothered against mortality. Mortality against me. Me against movement. Movement against many. Many against mediocrity. Mediocrity against mouth. Mouth against morality. Morality against mediocrity. Mediocrity against mediocrity.

Hoping for the hope of transcendence. The hope of death against life. The hope for immortality.

But what they didn't count on was this sharp eye seeing it all coming. They thought I wouldn't know what they had conspired for me. I could see it in their jaundiced, cynical eyes. They would feed me in and use me. Filter me through the system, knowing I would go for the ascendant position, take my name and put it down everywhere I could. Lay the seeds of my thoughts and snatch victory from the teeth of failure. And take it all away from me again.

But I could do it, despite the hands and feet kicking, punching at my head.

What they wanted I could give them, but I refused. If it were down to them, they would have me become the monster they wanted, become the beast that battled in their name. But I out-thought them, outsmarted them to the last moment. The Old Man and her, pushing me toward greatness but holding me on a tether, ready to wrench my spine out of my withered flesh at the moment of triumph. Put me in, turn me their way, Metropolis's way, then unmask me as the mark, the patsy for their political ends.

The kidnapper. The drug addict. The monster. Their ideology, as much a delusion as the worst and most putrid minds.

An experiment, a control and a rat. Sonntag and his creation pitted in the dust, turned face to face. Hand to hand.

But I played them. The game turned its thick neck and revealed the beast's head. They had planned it for me that day, the capture. The training and my teaching. Seeing through it, I knew the game was up for them. I would be protected by my new mentors. They would guide me through the tunnel and hand it all to me when I called upon them.

The templates. The words. The feeling and the fact.

CHAPTER FOUR

I took my usual place on the sofa. I opened the tall bottle, allowing the yellow brew's odour to escape. After heavy and repeated usage, the nausea lessens until it dies away completely. Then there are only the visions.

To be able to see without eyes. That would certainly be a way forward. They had all been great and almost blind, most of them. After all, we all go blind eventually. But they held the Insight even when the eyeballs failed.

Huxley, born 1894, died 1963, age 69

Dostoevsky, born 1821, died 1881 = 59

Kierkegaard, born 1813, died 1855 = 42

Rimbaud, born 1854, died 1891 = 37

Camus, born 1913, died 1960 = 46

Hamsun, born 1859, died 1852 = 92

Fante, born 1909, died 1983 = 74

Celine, born 1894, died 1961 = 67

Villon, born 1431, died 1463 = 32

Hemingway, born 1899, died 1961 = 61

Nabokov, born 1899, died 1977 = 78

Anderson, born 1876, died 1941 = 64

Miller, born 1891, died 1980 = 88

Bakunin, born 1814, died 1876 = 62

Vonnegut, born 1922, died 2007 = 84

Nietzsche, born 1844, died 1900 = 55

Lautréamont, born 1846, died 1870 = 24

Conrad, born 1857, died 1924 = 66

Tzara, born 1896, died 1963 = 67

Dick, born 1928, died 1982 = 53

Musil, born 1880, died 1942 = 61

Whitman, born 1819, died 1892 = 72

Burroughs, born 1914, died 1997 = 83

Bukowski, born 1920, died 1994 = 73

Burgess, born 1917, died 1993 = 76

Thompson, born 1937, died 2005 = 67

Kafka, born 1883, died 1924 = 40

Zamyatin, born 1884, died 1937 = 53

Pound, born 1885, died 1972 = 87

Average: 63.17

They all went blind in the end. Impaired vision before that.

There was something in the power the mind had, and the way it saw, that meant their vision had to suffer. Maybe because of it. Maybe not.

The smoke moved up against the glass. The window, shut. Samstag watched where he always watched. He moved his head from side to side, angling it and improving the view. The leaves moved across his vision. He sighed.

He stood up and looked down to the street. A truck. A man with a chainsaw. Dust flew up out of the base of the trunk. A gnawing sound jarred him where he stood. The man cut it first at the tip where it lay dangling over the windshield of a parked car. The rest of its branches flayed out and scraped the side windows.

As Samstag watched, the man removed the first piece and laid it by the side of the road. The leaves that had obscured his vision most, Samstag now watched the man take care of them. He imagined going down there and taking the first stumps and waving them around, swinging them and smashing them on the pavement. A part of him would still be in a rage if that tree survived somewhere, somehow. Somehow it would always haunt his memory. He looked at his hand and noticed that he was shaking. His hand trembled as he raised it closer to the eye. A splinter. The thumb too. It had bled across the floor. Wrinkled and dry, pale and shrivelled he put it up to his nose. He sat, suddenly weakened. Deep in his seat. He lit a cigarette and watched the window from the low view in the chair. The white of the cigarette soaked through, the colour of beetroot.

The leaves left on the tree, the part that bent over and refused to break, waved and clawed at his window. A screeching of wood against glass. Fingernails on the blackboard. Blank. In the face of it. A blank.

There was a great whirring below in the street. Chainsaw through tree. It would be the last few inches of that bastard trunk that refused to give way. A small police barrier had been put up and three officers watched and talked. They never looked up. Not once. He sucked in the smoke, soaking the butt, feeling it crawl its yellow and its puss out, blood smearing across his lip. He held the thumb high and stared at it.

The window across glinted. A light flickering on. No faces. No bodies. Just the light coming on.

Samstag thought to himself. He wondered where they were hiding. He wondered why his obsession had not yet yielded. When he felt the first tear find its way down his cheek he lifted the pale thumb and let the moisture soak in the cracked blood. It was dark, purple as he looked at it. As it connected with the tears, it turned a deep red. A dark, healthy red. A red as deep as summer. A red as deep as autumn. A red as deep as winter. A red as deep as spring.

The tears flowed. The long nails on his fingers scratched underneath his eyes. Black and tired. Above the house he could see the pure white of the sky. They were clouds but glowing white, the enemy sun behind them, somewhere. Black was the roof, running below the white sky. As it ran in his sight, cutting the white, he saw a crow. No. A pigeon. No. Something smaller. Something moving as if dying. It moved along the horizon of black on white, dragging its dead self along. It held something tight in its mouth. Its beak. Whatever it was. Samstag watched it as it refused to let go. Holding onto the windowsill with four feeble fingers, he leaned forward and stared out through the stream in his eyes. Bouncing slowly along the black roof it leapt from tile to tile. He thought he saw a worm in its mouth. He felt it wriggling in his own.

The loud slicing of blade through tree jaggedly echoed up the edifices of the old buildings. In between, the sound reflected back and forth. Off stone. Off glass. Off their eyes. The old buildings that had survived wars. The trophies of history sitting atop them, turn-of-the-century stone sculptures. Samstag kept his eye on the creature still moving across. He begged that it would take off, at least die elsewhere. Out of his sight, out of his mind.

As Samstag stood up to the window, the blinds across flickering, he did not notice the frenzied activity in the opposite apartment. The blinds shook and the window bent with a blow by flesh, items tossed in the air and against the mirrors, cracking them, making them fall and smash.

Samstag. The creature. It made its way. As it bounced to the centre tile atop the roof, a claw slipped. The worm in the mouth let fly and tumbled down the tiles, whipping its body over itself again and again. Hitting the black piping running beneath, it dangled on the edge, its weight gradually tipping it over, sending it down, reaching terminal velocity as it flashed past window and window. A tiny slap on the pavement.

The creature's slip had not yet been recovered. It lay there trying to recover its weight, jack-knifed on the top of the roof. It flapped a turgid, useless wing. Only one of them worked. It let out a shrill yell as it attempted to help itself up. On its belly it struggled. A flap of the ripped wing. A muted screech.

The tears were still falling out of the corners of Samstag's eyes when the creature began its silent descent. As the worm before it, the creature rolled over itself, limp and helpless. Turning over and over itself, a piece of black matter tumbling. Down the wet tiles, sliding down. Collapse. Into death. It disappeared off the edge of the black pipe.

The creature's lifeless body ceased to spin as it hurtled downward through the air. A vision. Still. Plummeting.

As the chainsaw worked up to cut the final stubborn piece of trunk away from its mother, a louder slap hit the pavement. The policemen did not notice. They continued stories with gesticulations and coffees. Of nights before and days coming. His head dropped.

Samstag moved away from the window. Slowly bending his knees he laid a hand down first and lowered the rest of his weight onto the floor. He sat in his dry blood. Tears down the face. To the precipice. The chin. Off the edge.

He moved over to his desk, crawling, ignoring the scene of the street, the cutting of the wood, the people across, the policemen below, the call of the sun and he stood by. On his knees, looking down, he lifted the biro. The one he had scribbled with for all that time. Holding it in his fist he ran it across the page and drew large Xs on the sheets in front of it. X over the whole page. He turned a leaf and scored that too. Throwing the sheet at his feet he did the next page and the next. The pen ran itself dry as it reached the corner of the ninth sheet. He looked at the tip. A strong grip in the middle of his balled fist. He picked up another pen, a fresh one, and removed the lid. He looked at both the tips, holding them close to his eyes, analysing the gold nibs, the dribble of ink that ran over one of them, and the emptiness of the other. In both his fists he held the two pens. Drawing them closer to his head he watched them move in on his sight and out of focus.

Both pens slid into his eye sockets simultaneously. He quietly pushed them back toward the brain, all the way up to his fists. Slow. The dark red began to drip down his cheeks and into his mouth.

His arms now weak, they lowered toward his chest, still gripping the plastic. They angled up toward the top of his skull and the red dribbled down from the eye to the finger then down his palms and along his arm. His legs gave way and he tumbled back into the wall and slid down, still holding on to the drenching redness. He sat there. Motionless. The corners of his lips turned down.

In agony, he found my self in the apartment across.

My Self. Sat on the floor.

A dead body leaking greasy red out from under. A long split in the corpse's side. Her swollen stomach ruptured. Bleeding. Only a thick wooden handle visible, the blade deep up to the cheek.

He was Alone.

Alone.

Waiting.

A strange, new kind of guilt.

The sounds of the avenue flooding back. Footsteps in the stairway. The rain had stopped.

(EXT. NIGHT)

He reached his hand up to the glass, on the sill lay the final cigarette. He smiled.

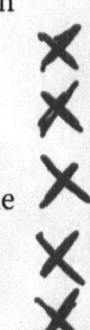

(INT. NIGHT)

I waited. Knowing. The dark arms arriving.

(EXT. NIGHT)

He ended it.
Motionless.
Alive.

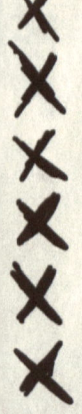

EPILOGUE

I looked up into the sky. A heavy gray pregnant with rain. I lit the last cigarette.

Think. I'd been kicked out or I'd left. I couldn't remember which.

Imagining her sitting up there, breathing in her fine cigarettes, stiff and ignoring emotion. The red stream and broken smoke.

She said she couldn't stand me for my inconsistency. I said: one is not the same throughout the day. One cannot be. One should not be.

Stood in the breeze craning my neck to see, I waited. Taking whatever angle I could to subsist. I spied it through the unborn limbs of the cherry blossom, the window shifting through the branches all emptied of leaves.

It would be the end of me.

The view of the aged edifice remained flat. Cold. Solid and dead. I had no tricks to disregard that. I could deceive my self, particularly to those little things. Completely. No question.

The gray climbed and swayed between the clouds. Like her it gleamed without remorse. I waited outside

for something to happen. A signal from the window. A solemn face. Some gesture of regret. I hoped that maybe she might change her mind.

I had waited there for a long time. Not realising there was nothing left in her to change.

As the widening jaw of the high streets and parades swallowed the braces and metal bound to my wrists.

I was marched farther away from it, and into the closing city.

METRO POLIS

Committed to Liberty, Integrity and Equality.

The unbiased, objective voice: of reason, of logic, of passion, of justice.

I live my values and so does my audience.

I pledge to be impartial, fair, accurate, balanced and independent.

Freedom, Fairness and Responsibility.

Democracy is the root of my service.

Like the intellectual mind, I am an institution that watches my Self.

Without Metro Polis, my life would be impoverished, my knowledge diminished.

Without Metro Polis, I would be threatened by social and political catastrophe.

Through these virtues, I protect the people with bravery and tenacity.

And I always will.

Power is given only to those who dare to lower themselves
and pick it up.

– Dostoyevsky, *Crime and Punishment*

We hope you've enjoyed the story. Please help us share this story with other readers by letting us know what you thought with a review on either **amazon.com** or **goodreads.com**.

Thank you kindly,
Montag Press Collective

Acknowledgements

Thank you to my parents. Thank you to Alex Paskulin. Thank you to Charlie. Thank you to Arno. Thank you to Badger. Thank you to Justin. And thank you to V.

Declan Tan worked as a journalist. This was his first book.